His Kingdom

Owning Vegas

kylie Kent

ISBN 13: 978-1-923137-69-1 ebook)
978-1-923137-72-1 (paperback)

Cover Illustration by Cover Kate Farlow – Y'all That Graphic

Edited By
Kat Pagan

Club Omerta

Are you a part of the Club?

Don't want to wait for the next book to be released to the public?
Come and Club Omerta for an all access pass!

This includes:
- daily chapter reveals,
- first to see - everything, covers, teasers, blurbs
- Advanced reader copies of every book
- Bonus scenes from the characters you love!
- Video chats with me (Kylie Kent)
- and so much more

Click the link to be inducted to the club!!!
CLUB OMERTA

Chapter One

She's coming back. She will come back for me. My mom. She always comes back for me. I don't know how long she's been gone now. My stomach hurts. I'm hungry. But I don't dare move from this spot, because I need to be here when she comes back.

"Stay right there, Louie. I'll be back as soon as I

finish work and then we can go and get the biggest burger and fries," Mom said.

I think about that burger. I wonder if Mom will get me a milkshake too? I won't ask for it, though. My mom gets sad when I ask for things and she can't buy them. One day, I'm going to have enough money to buy her everything, so she never has to be sad again.

A flashlight shines over the end of the dark alley. I huddle myself farther back. My mom left me between two dumpsters. She said I'd be warmer if I stayed out of the wind. Las Vegas is in the desert. Which means it's always warm during the day and cool at night.

Heavy footsteps get closer and closer until the beam of light is blinding me, and my eyes scrunch closed.

"It's okay. You can come out. We're here to help you," a man's voice says.

Mom told me I should never trust any man but myself. She said they're all liars and cheats. So I don't move.

"It's okay. Come on out, little man. Let's get you something to eat." A lady's voice has me opening my eyes. I can trust a lady, right? Mom didn't say not to trust ladies. Just men.

"I can't leave. My mom is coming back for me," I reply.

6

"Do you know your mom's name? We can help you look for her," the lady says.

"It's Maria. And I don't have to look because she's coming back."

"Okay, let me take you down to the station and we can look for your mom." The lady doesn't seem to understand.

"Will my mom be in trouble?" Police mean trouble. They don't always help. I know that. I've seen lots of Mom's friends get taken away by the police.

"No, she's not going to be in trouble."

I push myself to my feet and walk towards the lady. I'm weak. I don't know how long I've been here. I kept falling asleep and waking up.

"Good boy. Let's get you warm, and then we can get you something to eat," the lady tells me.

I wake up from the recurring nightmare. Hungry. Starving actually. Just like I was that day, and many days after it. So I get up out of bed and head into the kitchen. The fridge is full of ready-made fresh meals. My housekeeper ensures it's always fully stocked.

I made a promise to myself the moment I found out my mother was never coming back for me that I was going to one day have so much money, my own house, and my own fridge full of food. I promised myself I'd never go hungry again. And still, every fucking day, I wake up starving, as if I haven't eaten in a week.

I pull out a container of pasta and throw it in the microwave. While it's heating up, I walk back into my room and retrieve my phone. I open the app that controls the blinds and hit the button that lets the light flow into the penthouse. It's three in the afternoon. But when you work nights, you sleep days. Or at least try to sleep anyway.

The microwave dings, and I grab the pasta and set it on the counter as I delete the first few messages that aren't important. I don't have time to waste on bullshit. Running this city takes all of my time. Being a king isn't for the weak—that's for fucking sure. And in this city, Las Vegas, the city of sin, I am the king.

I rule with an iron fist too. Nothing happens that I don't know about. I worked my ass off to reach the top of the food chain, and I don't plan on letting anyone kick me off my throne.

I open a message from Sammie; he's one of the two men I let close enough to call friends. After all, a king doesn't reign alone. He always has his court, and just like any good ruler, I have carefully chosen the men who work for me.

SAMMIE:

Bossman, a delivery just came in for you.

My lips tip up as I read his message. When Sammie has a delivery for me at Wild Card, it usually means he's got a bunch of women holed up in the VIP room. I own three casinos here on the strip: Royal Flush, Wild Card, and Aces High. Sammie runs the Wild Card and Carlo, the other lucky bastard I let into my circle, handles Aces High.

ME:

A delivery? Did you pay for it?

I laugh, counting down the seconds for Sammie's reply. He has a thing about paying for pussy, says he never has and never will. I don't know what his hangup with prostitutes is, but he can't stand them.

SAMMIE:

Fuck no. I don't need to pay for pussy.

ME:

I got a few things to tie up here. Be over in an hour.

Standing up, I pocket my phone, grab my wallet and keys from the desk, and reach a hand around my back until my fingers run over my pistol. I know it's there, but checking is just like breathing at this point. Then I walk out of my office and head down to the casino floor. I make it a habit to walk the floor every night. It's good to be seen by my staff. It helps them maintain the fear of god. Because to them, that's exactly who I am. Their god.

It takes me almost an hour to make my way through the high rollers, stopping to talk to regulars and business associates. As much as I have my feet in the underworld of Vegas, I also have a solid interest in the legitimate workings of the business. Playing both sides of the coin is crucial... and fucking exhausting. It's why at least once a week, I allow myself a few hours to sink into some hot, willing pussy. Which is exactly what I plan to do tonight.

I don't usually pay too much attention to the general area of the casino, but something catches my eye—or more like *someone*. I stop walking as I take her in. Fucking gorgeous. Long, brown curls hang loose over her shoulders. A skintight black lace dress hugs all of her curves. The kind of curves I could get lost in for days. Then there's the face. Angelic. Thick lips and big, round eyes that have the saddest look in them. But it's not just sadness. It's loneliness. I recognize it, because I feel it every fucking day I wake up.

My feet move before I realize what I'm doing. Stepping towards her. I stop one of the drink girls. "How long has she been sitting there?" I ask, not taking my eyes off the woman.

"I don't know. She was there when I clocked in four hours ago. You need anything, boss?" the girl says.

"Yeah, bring me a whiskey and whatever she's been drinking."

"Water. She's been drinking water," the girl tells me before walking off.

The woman startles when I sit in the seat opposite her. She's in a booth, at the back of one of the main floor bars. I bet she was thinking she wouldn't be seen in this dark corner. The thing with me, though, is I live in the dark. Thrive in it. And an angel like this does not belong here with me.

"Was this seat taken?" I ask her.

She glances from side to side, as if she's looking for someone else I could be talking to. "No," she finally says, peering back in my direction. And when her eyes connect with mine, I see so much hurt. Pain that I want to erase from her. Which is fucking weird. I don't even know this chick's name.

"I'm Louie. You are?" I hold out my hand to her.

"Charlotte," she says quietly as she places her palm in mine. The moment my skin touches hers, I get hit with jolts of electricity running up my arm. Charlotte snatches her hand back, staring down at it with wonder.

Yeah, I felt that too, I think to myself.

"So, what brings you to Sin City, Charlotte?" I ask, loving how her name rolls off my tongue.

"I'm in mourning," she says with a slight southern twang.

"I'm sorry for your loss," I tell her. Everyone deals with grief differently, but not many come to Vegas to do it.

"Don't be. It's probably for the best."

"Mind if I ask who you're mourning?"

"Does it matter?" she counters.

"Well, kind of, yeah. You see, if it was someone close like a spouse, child, parent, or sibling... that calls for some deep mourning, and that shit takes time. If it was a distant relative or a friend, that calls for getting drunk and honoring their memory," I tell her.

Charlotte looks at me, unblinking for a minute and a half. I know because I count the seconds. "What if it's a fiancé and a sister?" she finally asks.

"You lost your fiancé *and* your sister?" No wonder she's so fucking sad. "What happened?"

"The word *lost*... It means something is gone, taken, unrecoverable." She looks away for a moment and I wait. When she looks back at me, it's with so much hurt that I feel her pain. "My fiancé took my sister from me."

"What do you mean?" I keep my voice calm. I'm ready to blow the head off whoever the fuck hurt this girl.

"I mean, I walked in on my fiancé and sister fucking yesterday," Charlotte says. "He could have picked anyone, any girl, and he picked my sister. Why would he do that?" Her question is genuine, as if I have the answers she so desperately needs.

"Any man who cheated on you, sweetheart, is a fucking idiot," I say, because if I had a woman like her, no way would I stray.

"I was supposed to get married today. Right now, I should be at the reception dinner my father paid a small fortune for. Instead, I'm hiding because I can't face the truth."

"Well, you're not very good at hiding, sweetheart. I found you."

"Boss, whiskey and water." The drink girl comes up and sets the glasses down in front of me.

"Thank you." I hand her a hundred, and she walks away. I push the water towards Charlotte and hold up my own glass. "I am sorry for what you're feeling. But there's always another side to the coin, sweetheart. By finding them before you signed up for life, you dodged a bullet. You could have spent the next ten years not knowing the person you were married to. Now, you get to start over. Find happiness. Find someone who deserves you."

"Boss? Why did she call you *boss*?" Charlotte questions.

"I own this place." I wave a hand around the bar.

"The bar? That's cool. Must be exciting work."

"The casino. What do you do?" I ask, and Charlotte laughs.

"I *was* a personal assistant. I quit my job. Two weeks ago. Owen wanted to start a family right away. He wanted me to be at home."

"Owen sounds like a tool," I grunt.

Charlotte's eyes water. She's fighting hard not to cry. "You really own this whole casino? Does that mean you can, like, grant me access to the roof pool even though it's shut?"

"You wanna go swimming? I can make that happen."

"I want to drown in the water instead of the hurt," she whispers, and I can only hope she doesn't mean literally.

I quickly down the rest of my whiskey, push to my feet, and hold out my hand. "Come on, I'll take you swimming, but I'm not letting you drown. In water *or* hurt."

Chapter Two

Twenty four hours earlier

No matter what I do, I'm going to hurt someone. If I go one way, I hurt my fiancé, my family, and friends who supported us throughout our relationship. Those who followed our journey to get here. If I go the other, I hurt myself.

I've weighed both sides of the situation. If I hurt my fiancé, he'll likely move on. He'll find happiness with someone else. He's not a bad guy. He's just not the guy for me. On the other hand, I could go through with this, marry Owen, and spend the rest of my life dying a little on the inside each day.

I don't know when it happened, if it was instant or something that grew over time. How I fell out of love with my fiancé, or maybe I wasn't ever really in love with him in the first place. I've been with Owen for two years. Six months ago, he proposed in front of everyone. I said yes, because in the moment, I thought it was everything I'd ever wanted. Now, the night before I'm supposed to walk down the aisle, I'm not so sure.

I've made up my mind. I decided to choose *me*. If that makes me the most selfish asshole on the planet, then so be it. But with each step I take, I'm doubting my choice. Maybe I just need to see him. My mind will clear itself up if we just sit down and have a conversation, work it out together. I can do that. We can do that.

When I reach his hotel room, I swipe the entrance card against the panel and push the door open. As soon as I step inside the suite, I hear the noise. The unmistakable noise of sex. My heart drops, but my feet... they keep moving towards the bedroom.

Until I'm standing on the threshold, staring in horror as I watch my fiancé fuck my sister. I don't know how long I stand here. They don't even notice that I'm watching. Without thinking, I pick up my phone and hit record. No one is going to believe me if I don't have proof.

After obtaining a decent amount of footage, I walk out of the room. Out of the hotel. I don't know where I'm going, but I find myself in my car and then I'm at the airport.

I need to be alone. I need to go somewhere no one will find me.

Staring up at the board of flights, I read through the list of cities. Las Vegas. I've never been there, but if what all the movies say is true, no one will find me. Also, it's the last place my family will think to look for me.

I walk up to the counter and plaster on my best smile. It's not this poor woman's fault that I'm having a shitty day. "Hi, is there any chance I can get on that Vegas flight?" I ask her.

"Let me have a look," she says, tapping away at her keyboard.

"Thank you. I really appreciate it," I tell her.

She looks up and offers me a smile. "We have a seat. Economy okay?"

"More than okay. Thank you so much." I sigh in relief as I hand her my credit card and ID.

"Not a problem at all." She takes my card, and five minutes later, she's giving me a boarding pass. "Do you have any luggage to check?"

"Ah, no, I didn't bring anything." *Shit, that sounds lame.* Who goes on a trip without any bags?

"Let me see that boarding pass. I made an error." The lady takes the ticket out of my hand, goes back on her computer, and then another boarding pass is being printed. "Oh, look at that! You've received a complimentary upgrade, Miss Armstrong," she says before handing me a new pass. "You look like you could use it."

"Thank you," I choke out, trying not to cry. *I will not cry.*

It's not like I one hundred percent wanted to marry Owen. I did one hundred percent want to grow old with my sister, though. How am I ever supposed to look her in the eye again? How am I supposed to trust her? What kind of sister does that?

Once I'm on the plane, I lean my head back. *I won't cry,* I remind myself. I don't really deserve to cry. I was going there to break up with him... I think. The funny part is I'm more hurt over my sister's betrayal than Owen's. I don't know what I'm supposed to do. I look down at my phone. I should tell someone, maybe message my parents to let them know there won't be a wedding...

Instead, I do something that's totally unlike me. It's vengeful and unexpected.

I send my sister a message, telling her how I want to make a grand surprise entrance, that I'm getting ready alone at another hotel and that I'd meet them at the door. I've been picturing Owen's face all day when he realizes I'm not showing up. That he was left standing at the altar. I know how embarrassed he'll be, and that makes me smile a little.

Screw the cheating, sister-stealing bastard. I just wish I was there to see it.

I'm sure I look like I feel right now. I didn't sleep. I spent the night crying and maybe plotting the hypothetical death of my ex-fiancé. I thought up all sorts of bloody and painful ways I could take him out. Obviously, I'd never actually do it. Like I said, it was all hypothetical.

As soon as I landed, I got an Uber and came here to the Royal Flush. I didn't put too much thought into where I was going to stay. I picked the first casino on the strip that came up on Google search. And that brings me to right now, sitting in front of a guy who claims to own this casino. Not just a guy. A god. Insanely gorgeous. Chiseled jaw, dark green eyes, brown hair that's cut short and styled neat. He's wearing a suit that looks expensive, judging by the way the fabric molds to his body. A body I'm sure would be all hard lines and angles if I were to touch it. Not that I have any intention of touching him. But I'm not going to say no if he really can get me into the closed pool.

"Really? We can go in the pool?" There's something about swimming that's always been therapeutic for me. Being weightless in the water is just freeing. Right now, I could use that more than anything.

Louie stands and holds out a hand for me. "Let's go swimming."

I place my palm on his as I push up from the booth. He doesn't drop my hand like I expected him to. No, he continues to hold it as he leads me through the casino to the bank of elevators. He hits the button for the rooftop and swipes a card. I look down at our joined palms. There's a comfort in his touch that I don't understand. I'm probably delusional. I'm running on no sleep and a whole lot of coffee. There is no way I'm getting comfort from a complete stranger.

"You're not a serial killer, are you?" I ask him.

Louie coughs as he stares down at me. "Not the last time I checked. Are you?"

"No." I shake my head. "I faint at the sight of blood and gore, so even if I wanted to, I'd suck at it."

"There are plenty of ways to kill someone without making them bleed," Louie tells me.

"Such as?"

"You planning on offing me, Charlotte?" he asks with a smile.

"Not you, no," I reply.

Louie looks at me—trying to read me, no doubt—until the doors open, breaking us out of our little staring contest. "Let's swim," he says.

The smell of chlorine hits me the moment we step out onto the rooftop. The air is warm, and there is no one else here. The water glistens with the reflection of the city lights. "This is amazing. Are you sure we're not going to get in trouble for being up here?"

"How? Ain't no one going to say shit to me, Charlotte." Louie takes off his jacket and tie, placing them neatly over one of the pool chairs. Then he unfastens his cufflinks and pockets them before folding the sleeves of his dress shirt up to his elbows. "Are you getting in?" he asks before sitting on one of the lounge seats by the edge of the pool.

"Are you?" I counter.

He shakes his head. "I'm just here to make sure you don't drown, Charlotte. Go ahead. Jump in."

I look down at the simple dress I'm wearing. I don't have a bathing suit. I went to the store today and bought some of the basics to tide me over for a couple of days. "Underwear is basically the same thing as a bikini, right?" I say as I pull my dress over my head. Then I slip my feet out of my shoes and kick them aside.

Louie's eyes travel over my body. I'm wearing a matching lace bra and panty set. I probably should have thought about this a bit more, but I really want to swim and a lack of a bathing suit is not going to stop me. I tie my hair up into a messy bun on top of my head, then sit on the side of the pool and drop into the water.

24

I turn to face Louie and find him staring right back at me. "It's really nice. Sure you don't want to jump in?" I ask him.

"I'm good," he says.

"Suit yourself, but just so you know, you're missing out." I sink under the water and close my eyes. I stay under for as long as I can. When I come back up for air, Louie is crouched down at the side of the pool.

"What the fuck, Charlotte? I was about to jump in and pull you up," he grunts.

"Why?" My brows crease together.

"Because I thought you were... Just don't do that again. Keep your head above water." He stands and reclaims his seat.

"Sorry," I mumble. "I didn't mean to scare you."

"You didn't," he says, looking away from me.

"Right."

The proper thing to do right now would be to get out of the pool and let this man get back to doing whatever it was he was doing before he sat down at my table. I don't do that, though. Instead, I turn around and start swimming laps.

Chapter Three

Louie

There's something about this woman that's pulling me towards her. My brain is telling me to get up and walk away. Let her swim to her heart's content and leave her alone. My body, though... it wants to do everything but that.

I'm itching to jump into the pool, press her up against the wall, and sink my cock so deep into her pussy she won't remember she was supposed to get married today. What kind of fucking idiot cheats on a woman like that? *Like her.* I can't fathom it. If she were mine, she'd never have to worry about me even looking at another woman.

She can't be mine, though. She's too sweet, inno-cent, kind. She does not belong in the world I live in. She'd get eaten alive. She'd become a target—some-thing my enemies could use against me.

One of the reasons I've never been in a relation-ship is so I don't have any weaknesses. I've also never met a woman I've wanted to keep longer than a night. I'm not saying I want to keep Charlotte longer than a night, but I'm not sure I don't want to keep her either.

My phone buzzes in my pocket. I pull it out while not taking my eyes off her. She's swimming laps, continuous laps. Surely she's going to wear herself out soon. Looking down, I open the message on my screen.

SAMMIE:

Bossman, you got a heartbeat still?
If not, I better be in your will. Where
the fuck are you?

28

Fuck, I was supposed to meet up with him an hour ago. I got distracted. And Charlotte is a distraction I'm not ready to get rid of.

ME:

Rooftop pool. I'm taking a pass on tonight.

I pocket my phone and go back to watching Charlotte. She wasn't shy at all when it came to stripping down in front of me. I think her need to swim overrode any objections she might have had about getting nearly naked in front of a stranger.

When she comes back to the shallow end of the pool, she stops and looks up at me, her chest heaving as she takes a moment to catch her breath. "You should try this. You look tense and the water always eases my stress," she says.

"I'm good." I don't tell her I'm tense because my mind is focused on trying to figure out if I can get away with fucking the sadness out of her eyes.

"You don't have to babysit me, you know. I'm sure you have other things to do." She looks away, and I follow her gaze to the strip.

I own this fucking town. Taking time out to sit by a pool isn't something I've ever done. And yet, here I fucking am.

"Tonight just happens to be my night off. I've got no other plans." I smile. "Besides, I'm happy to sit here and look at the view."

"It is pretty," she says, staring out at all the lights.

"It's fucking breathtaking," I reply, staring right at her.

Charlotte's cheeks turn pink. It's a faint change, and I'm sure I'd be able to see the flush in them more if I were closer. The sound of the door opening has me standing, ready to deal with whatever asshole managed to get up here without a damn pass.

And then Sammie saunters over. "Boss, not like you to go for a midnight swim." He smiles and looks behind me. At Charlotte. "Ah, I think I see the appeal now."

"Get your eyes off her." I walk up to where he's standing and grunt in a low voice so only he can hear me. Then I walk behind him so he's forced to turn around. "What are you doing here?" I ask him.

"Checking up on your MIA ass," he says.

"Well, now that you've seen I'm fine, you can leave." I nod my head in the direction of the door.

"Sure." Sammie smirks. "Right after I meet your friend." He pivots on a heel and strolls towards the pool again.

How much would it bother Charlotte if I drowned this fucker in the water right next to her?

"Hey there. I'm Sammie, and you are?" My soon-to-be-dead friend holds out his hand.

Before Charlotte reaches out to take it, I walk over and knock Sammie into the water. Then I bend down, pick Charlotte up, and drag her out of the pool. "Sorry about that. He looked like he wanted to sink." I smirk.

"Fucker." Sammie laughs when his head pops up for air. His eyes on Charlotte, who is wearing nothing but wet underwear.

"Turn the fuck around," I tell him.

"Fine. Let me know when you two kids are decent," Sammie says, holding his hands in the air in a surrender motion.

I grab my jacket and wrap it around Charlotte's shoulders before I pick up one of the towels and pull the tie out of her hair. Letting it fall in long, wet curls down her back. I wrap the towel around her hair and dry it off the best I can.

Charlotte is as stiff as a board. I look down at her, tilting her chin upwards so she has to make eye contact with me. "You okay?" I ask, while using the corner of the towel to gently wipe the droplets of water from her face.

"Mhmm. I should get back to my room. Thank you for letting me swim," she says.

"I'll walk you," I tell her before calling over a shoulder, "Sammie, get out of the pool."

"You really don't need to walk me back to my room," Charlotte says.

"I really do," I insist. "This city is full of drunk asses and, frankly, undesirable men who would take one look at you like this and... Well, you get the point."

"Um, thank you. I'm sorry I took up your time," she replies as the elevator doors close.

"What floor?" I ask her, swiping my access card over the panel.

"Five."

We're both silent as we descend to the fifth floor before the doors open again, and I follow Charlotte until she stops in front of room 527. She unlocks the door, and I wait for her to turn around. "Are you going to be okay?" I ask her.

"I'm going to be fine. I'm a southern girl. Nothing keeps us down. Tomorrow I'm going to put on my lipstick, straighten my shoulders, and move on as if nothing happened. Tonight, I'm going to grieve the loss of my sister," she says.

"I understand that everything is fresh. Feelings

are... intense. But your sister isn't dead, Charlotte. Shitty, definitely. But she's not dead."

"She is to me." Charlotte shrugs. "Oh, your jacket."

When she starts to remove it, I place a hand on her shoulder to stop her. "Keep it. And just so you know, your ex is a fucking idiot for losing you."

"Thank you."

"Good night, Charlotte."

"Good night, Louie," she says before closing the door.

I take my phone out of my pocket and quickly call down to the lobby. "Good evening, Mr. Giuliani. How may I help you?" a young girl answers.

"There's a woman in room 527... Have her upgraded to penthouse two, on the house. For two weeks. Tell her she's won an all-expenses-paid extension," I direct the girl.

"Okay, when would you like her moved?"

"Now." I cut the call as I enter the elevator. When I walk into my own suite, Sammie is waiting for me. Nothing but a towel wrapped around his waist. "Why the fuck are you naked in my apartment?" I ask him.

"Because some grouchy fucker pushed my ass into the pool." He points at me.

"You deserved it." Walking past him, I head for the wet bar by the window. The penthouse has views over the strip, the floor-to-ceiling glass now lit up with activity. I've always loved the hustle of this city.

"So, Charlotte? Where'd she come from and why are you hiding her?" Sammie asks.

"She's nobody, and I'm not hiding anyone." I turn and stare out the window.

"Nobody, huh? You never cared if I looked at an almost-naked *nobody* before," he counters.

"I was being respectful. You should try it some-time." My glass reaches my lips as Sammie's laugh echoes off the walls.

"Yeah, respectful, good one. When have you ever wanted to be respectful to a woman?" His hand slaps my shoulder.

"Don't touch me when you're fucking naked." I shove him aside, turn back to the wet bar, and refill my glass.

"I wouldn't be naked if I didn't get pushed in the fucking pool," he grunts.

"Is there an actual reason you're here?" I ask him.

"Yeah, asshole, it's called being a friend. *You should try it sometime,*" he snaps.

If anyone else spoke to me like that, they'd have a

bullet in their head before they could blink. Lucky for Sammie, he's one of the few people I actually tolerate.

"I've heard it's overrated," I tell him.

"Yeah, sure. Are you going to mope around here all night or come out?"

"I'm not moping, and I'm also not going out tonight," I say.

"Suit yourself." Sammie shrugs, and I think he's finally giving up and going to leave me in peace. "So, where'd Charlotte come from?"

My brows draw down at him. "Why are you so interested in Charlotte?"

"Because you are, so where'd you meet her?"

"Downstairs. She was sitting at the bar alone. I talked to her and she wanted to go swimming. It's not a big deal."

"Not a big deal? Okay, so you're just going around talking to random patrons and taking them swimming now?"

"It's my pool. If I want to let someone in it, I will. I also don't answer to you." I point a finger at him as the whiskey in my glass sloshes against the side of the crystal tumbler.

"Again, it's called being a friend." Sammie shakes his head. "I'm borrowing some clothes, since you destroyed mine." He walks off towards my bedroom, while I make my way into my office.

I don't know who this Charlotte is, but I'm intrigued enough to find out. So I fire up my laptop, log in to the guest details, and locate her reservation. It's easy to dig up information on people, but it's even easier when you have their full name, their date of birth, and their home address at your fingertips.

Chapter Four

Three blissful seconds. That's how long of a reprieve I got when I woke up. For three short seconds, I forgot where I was. I forgot why I'm here, and I forgot the image of my fiancé fucking my sister on the eve of our wedding.

My eyes burn with tears I refuse to let out. I will not let him reduce me to that girl. I'm going to take the weekend, and then I'll go home with my head held high.

Maybe... Or running away to Canada is always an option.

In a way, I should be grateful to Owen. He made my decision to call off the wedding not seem so self-ish. I really thought I'd be breaking his heart as well as the hearts of our family and friends who've supported us throughout our relationship. A relation-ship that I now know was nothing but a lie.

How long has he been sleeping with Melanie? And why did he have to pick *her*? My sister. Of all the women in our town, he chose my sister to cheat on me with. The last person I thought would ever do anything to hurt me. I can't remember a time where it wasn't Melanie and me against the world. We were as close as two sisters could get. Ride or die. Or at least I thought we were...

It hurts. Her betrayal.

My hand comes up and rubs against my chest, trying to ease the pain. It's pointless. This pain is too deep. Nothing is going to ease it.

The sound of a chiming doorbell startles me. I roll over and take in the room. Which isn't the same room I booked and paid for. This one is fancier than anything I could ever afford.

Not long after I got back to my *actual* room last night, I was told I won a free upgrade. I questioned the staff member. I mean, how could I win something when I didn't enter some sort of competition? And they just said that *it was my lucky night.*

When I tried to refuse the upgrade, the poor girl looked like she was going to vomit. She pleaded with me to accept it. I felt horrible. And honestly, I just wanted to sleep, and that is the only reason I caved and took the room I *didn't* win.

I have to admit it's a really nice suite, though.

The sound of the bell rings out again. So I drag myself off the bed, wrap the robe I discarded at the end of the mattress last night around my body, and make my way to the door. Where I'm met by a hotel staff member and a trolley. The smell of bacon hits me and my stomach growls. I didn't eat much of anything at all yesterday.

"Um, hi?" I question.

"Good morning, ma'am. I have your breakfast. Where would you like me to set it?" the young man asks.

"Ah... I didn't order anything. I think you have the wrong room," I tell him.

"It's complimentary, part of the package you won." He smiles at me expectantly.

"Are you sure?" Like I said, I don't know how I won anything and the lady from last night couldn't or wouldn't tell me how either. It's strange, but the smell coming from that cart is too hard to resist.

"Positive, ma'am. Where would you like it?" the guy asks again.

"Um, okay. Anywhere, I guess. Come in, let me find my purse for your tip," I reply as I step out of the doorway so he can enter.

"No need, ma'am." He places the plates covered in silver domes onto the dining table, and then proceeds to set up a placemat, a plate, cutlery, and glassware.

"Thank you."

With a nod of his head, the guy walks out and I'm left alone. In this luxurious room. With a table setting that looks suitable for royalty. I wonder if this is how Alice felt when she was in Wonderland. Because this is not normal. Well, not *my* normal anyway.

The silence is deafening. Being alone with my thoughts isn't what I need right now. I don't want to think about what I'm running from. I want to be lost in another world—someone else's world. I want to escape my reality. But first, I want to eat. The smells coming from the table are too good to ignore.

After stuffing myself with as much food as I could, I showered and threw on a shirt and a pair of cutoff shorts I purchased early yesterday. I came here with nothing but the clothes I was wearing. One of the first things I did was go and buy some essentials. Just enough for a couple of days. I can't hide forever.

I pick up my phone and turn it on. I need to tell my parents I'm okay. I'm surprised my face isn't all over the news outlets as a missing person yet. And the moment my screen comes alive, the notifications pour in. Missed calls, messages, emails. I skip past Owen and Melanie and click on my mom's message first.

I'd intended to let her know I was okay yesterday. I just didn't want to talk to anyone from back home. I should call her, explain everything. Then again, even if I tell her, she won't believe what I have to say, not unless she sees it for herself. Which is why I send her a message instead.

ME:

> I'm sorry for making you and Dad worry. I'm okay. I just need to take some time for myself. Please don't look for me or try to follow me. I'll come home soon. I promise. I had to leave. Owen and Melanie gave me no choice. I couldn't marry him after seeing this.

As soon as I hit send, I click on the video I took of my fiancé and sister and forward it to my mom. It's definitely not something any mother wants to see, her daughter having sex. But unless she witnesses it firsthand, I know Owen and Melanie will try to manipulate the situation in their favor or insist I got it wrong.

Clearly, they're good at lying. I wonder how long they've been going behind my back? I never told my sister about my doubts. I didn't tell anyone that I was doubting marrying Owen. I honestly thought it was wedding jitters and that I'd be fine come the day.

Now, I know I wasn't in love with him. I'm not heartbroken over his cheating. Embarrassed, yes. But my heart isn't breaking for Owen. It's breaking because I've lost my best friend, my sister. How can I ever trust her again after this? How can I look her in the face with the same respect I did a few days ago?

I can handle losing my fiancé. I was prepared to break it off myself. But Melanie... I'm not sure how I will go through the rest of my life without her. She's always been there. For every milestone, for every achievement, she was right by my side. Every heartbreak and hardship, she was the one who sat with me, the one who would always put me back together.

She's the one who is supposed to be here with me right now. To tell me what to do after discovering that my fiancé is cheating. After running out of my own wedding.

Who is going to be that person now?

My phone lights up with an incoming call. It's my mom. Pushing the button on the side, I power the device down. I can't talk to anyone right now. I'm not going to cry. And I know if I talk to my mom, *I'm going to cry.*

I throw my phone onto my bed, pick up the room card, and shove it in my back pocket. Then I walk out to the hall and towards the elevator. I have no idea where I'm going, but I feel like day-drinking is on the menu today. It's Vegas after all. You don't have to wait until five o'clock to start drinking here, right?

There's also the fact that absolutely no one knows me, so even if someone does see me day-drinking before noon, it won't matter. It can't ruin my reputation. Although, back home, I'm sure I'm going to be forever known as the runaway bride. The woman who broke Owen's heart.

Maybe that's better than the alternative. The version where the whole town knows my fiancé cheated on me with my sister. I can't drink in this casino, though. I don't want to chance running into *him* again. Louie. I've done my best not to think about the tall, dark, and *way* too good looking man who let me swim in the closed pool late last night.

He also sat and listened to me talk. And he didn't look like he was judging me. He said he owns the casino. If that's true, I'm sure he'll be around somewhere. Which is why I'm getting drunk *somewhere else*.

Walking down the strip, I dodge the crowds of people already partying. I guess it's not too early for me to start doing the same.

I don't want to venture too far. A few blocks down, a big neon sign in the shape of a playing card grabs my attention. Wild Card Casino. Looks like this is as good a place as any to drown my sorrows today.

Chapter Five

Louie

Obsession. An idea or thought that continually preoccupies a person's mind. I've been obsessed with two things in life: making money and ruling this city. And now, I think I might have found a third obsession that keeps intruding my thoughts. Charlotte.

I spent the night looking up everything I could

learn about her. I know where she grew up. I know the school she graduated from and that she was vale-dictorian. I know she has one sister, Melanie, and was engaged to be married this past weekend to an Owen Aiken, a sheriff in the small southern town she came from.

I know she broke her ankle in the eighth grade during cheer practice. I also know that she was admitted to the hospital a year ago when she miscar-ried at six weeks. She had chicken pox when she was five and her tonsils removed when she was seven.

I dug as deep as I could. She's clean as a whistle. Not a single parking ticket attached to her name. Charlotte Armstrong is the all-American girl next door. The type you take home to your mother. The same type I never would have let near my own mother.

As I've gotten older, the memories I had of the woman have turned from fun, loving, and playful to the reality of who and what she really was. A hooker. An addict who left her son alone in an alleyway while she went and overdosed on drugs. I mourned her for so long. And then one day I decided I was done. She didn't love me. If she did, she never would have left.

Although, if I didn't have the childhood I did, I

probably wouldn't be where I am today. So her leaving wasn't the worst outcome. Being alone isn't a bad thing. It's something you get used to and come to savor. If you don't have anyone you care about, you can't be hurt.

Which is why I need to cure myself of my latest obsession with Charlotte. I don't know what it is about the woman that I'm so drawn to. Yes, she's gorgeous but this is Vegas. The city is full of gorgeous women. Charlotte is just more... innocent. Perhaps that's the draw. Her innocence.

The only thing a man like me could do for a woman like that is break her. Destroy all the good she embodies. I don't know how I know she's good. I just do. In my position, you get real skilled at reading people, and I had Charlotte picked within minutes of sitting down at her table last night.

That's when I should have gotten up and walked away. Except I couldn't. Like I said, I'm fucking drawn to the woman, borderline obsessing over her. I know she's not in the casino. I watched her walk out and forced myself not to follow her.

For the last three hours, I've been holed up in my office, trying to get work done *without* thinking about her. Clearly that's going about as well as getting blood from a stone. I haven't looked her up again

kylie Kent

online, though. I'm not sure there's much more to find on her anyway.

I need a drink. I can't keep thinking about a woman I've met once. No woman has ever taken up this much of my time before.

The buzzing of my phone snaps my focus away from Charlotte when Sammie's name flashes across my screen. "Yeah?" I answer.

"Boss. You know the saying *don't shoot the messenger*, right?" he asks me.

"What happened?" I stand and grab my keys and wallet off the desk.

"Ah... yeah, maybe you should just come over to the Wild Card and see for yourself. The Four Suits bar," he says.

"What the fuck is going on, Sammie?" I grunt, already walking out of my office, and slam the door.

"Just get over here." He cuts the call before I can respond.

There are two people in this world who can get away with hanging up on me: Sammie and Carlo. The same two men I see when I walk into Four Suits ten minutes later. Each nursing a glass of amber liquid while neither appears to be on high alert. Which makes me wonder why the fuck I'm here.

"What's going on?" I direct my question to Sammie.

"That chick from last night... What was her name again?" he asks with a tilt of his head.

"Charlotte. What about her?" It takes more effort than I'd like to admit to keep my tone neutral. I don't need these fuckers giving me shit over being hung up on a woman.

"You said she doesn't mean fuck all to you, right?" Sammie smirks.

"I don't know her. Why would she mean anything? I've known you two assholes for fifteen years, and I'd put a bullet through either of you without blinking. What makes you think a woman I met for five minutes means shit?" I cross my arms over my chest and pin the fuckers with a glare.

"Nice to know you care." Carlo laughs, and I lift one shoulder in response.

"So, the fact that Charlotte is over there drunk as a skunk, surrounded by a group of guys plying her with more liquor than is good for her, doesn't bother you at all?" Sammi nods his head to the left.

I take my time to turn and look. And sure enough, Charlotte is sitting in a booth with three men. "Why should it bother me? I don't know her," I reply without taking my eyes off them.

"That's what I thought," he says. "Want a drink?"

I turn and glare at him. "No, I don't want a fucking drink," I grunt.

"Ah, shit. Boss, just remember... *public*. This bar is *very public* and you've got that murderous look going on right now." Carlo waves a hand at my face.

I shake my head and then I'm pivoting and walking over towards Charlotte before I can think better of it. I stop at her table and clear my throat, gaining the attention of the three guys surrounding her. I glare at the one sitting next to her. Blocking her exit from the booth. Blocking *my access* to her.

"Move," I tell him.

"We're good here," the fucker says.

"Oh boy, you shouldn't do that." I hear Sammie's voice behind me.

My hand clutches the asshole's collar and I lift him out of the booth. "I said move," I tell the guy before shoving him backwards. Then I turn back and hold out my hand towards Charlotte. "I've been looking for you," I lie.

"You have? Why?"

"We had plans to go swimming." Another lie. But I'll use whatever I can to get her to leave with me willingly. Though I'm not opposed to picking her up and dragging her out. It's not as if anyone is going to stop me.

"Swimming? Really? You're going to come with me this time?" she asks excitedly.

"Sure."

"Charlotte, do you know this guy?" one of the other fuckers in the booth asks.

"Mhmm, this is Louie. He's nice. And hot, right? Like how is a man allowed to be that good looking? I think if you strip off that suit, there's probably a manufacturer's warning on his skin," she says.

"A manufacturer's warning?" Carlo asks.

"Yep, like... *Caution! Don't stare for too long because your brain will turn to mush.* Or maybe... *Touch at own risk.* Because of, you know, how hot he is." Charlotte's eyes continue to roam over my body.

"Right." Carlo laughs.

"Charlotte, let's go." I reach down and pick up her hand, and she willingly slides out of the booth.

"Okay, swimming, right?" she asks, looking up at me while stumbling on her feet as she stands.

My arm wraps around her waist, steadying her. "Mhmm." I nod, having no intention of letting her near a damn pool when she's this wasted.

Charlotte's hand lands on my chest. Moving up and down. Patting me at the same time a smile spreads across her face. "You must work out a lot," she says.

"Come on, let's get out of here." I turn to leave and find my two friends standing there. Laughing.

"Nothing, huh?" Sammie raises his eyebrows at me.

"Shut the fuck up," I hiss at him.

"You need a hand?" Carlo asks.

"Yeah, get rid of those assholes." I dip my chin towards the booth, not letting go of Charlotte as we slowly make our way over to the bank of elevators.

"Are we swimming here?" she questions me. "Oh, I don't have my bathing suit! And I'm not wearing a bra," she whispers. Or at least I think *she thinks* she's whispering.

My eyes drift down to her chest, where her nipples are poking through the fabric of her shirt. *Fuck me, I shouldn't have looked.* Shifting my body, I shield hers from the eyes of any other fucker within peeking distance. *Fuck them. They don't get to see her like this.*

I want to go back to the bar and tear the eyes out of the heads of those jerks feeding her drinks. It's an irrational thought. And I don't know why I fucking care, but I do.

When the doors to the elevator open, I guide

Charlotte inside and press the button for the penthouse.

"Is P for pool?" she asks me.

"Penthouse," I tell her, and her eyes widen to saucers.

"There's a pool in the penthouse?"

"There is." *But she's not going in it.*

"How do you just go wherever you want? It's because you're hot, right? I've heard good-looking people get away with doing whatever they want," she rambles on.

"You know, if we're categorizing people as good looking, you'd land at the top of that list, Charlotte," I tell her.

She shakes her head. "Nope, not true. If that were true, my fiancé wouldn't have cheated on me with my sister," she says.

"Your *ex* is a fucking idiot," I reply, emphasizing the *ex* part, because I don't think I'm going to let her leave. At least not until I figure out why I'm so fixated on her, and what that means for me. And us.

Chapter Six

Y ou know when something is really delicious and so tempting that it goes without question that it's not good for you? Like an ice cream sundae, or a big bar of chocolate. Sure, it tastes good in the moment. But then you wake up and have to force yourself on that treadmill at the gym. And the regret hits you and you wish you didn't cave into temptation.

That's what Louie is. Temptation. A fine, tall, sexy, firm piece of temptation. He's also something I shouldn't want. That's the thing about wants, though. You don't *need* them. You just *want* them. And right now, I *really* want this man.

"It's been a very long time since I orgasmed." As soon as the words are out, I realize my internal thought just became an external one. My hand comes up, covering my mouth's betrayal, and my eyes widen.

Maybe he didn't hear me. There's a chance he didn't hear me, right?

"That's... How long exactly?" Louie asks, his eyes searing into mine.

"Forget I said that. I wasn't supposed to say that," I blurt out.

"How long?" he presses.

"Long enough that I don't even remember how good it was. I mean, I know it was good... I think..." I let my thoughts trail off. This is why I usually don't drink. I have no filter when I do.

"You think? Charlotte, if you *think* it was good, then you've never really orgasmed at all. Because if it were me, if I was the one getting you off, you'd remember that I shattered your entire fucking world. I wouldn't stop until I made sure of it." Louie's voice drops an octave. His hand on my waist tightens, and I swear I melt. Like I'm nothing but a puddle at this man's feet right now.

Then the doors to the elevator open. And without a word, Louie guides me into what has to be the penthouse. I'm doing my best to ignore what he just said, and when I walk farther into the room and spot the pool through a set of glass doors, I head that way. Maybe I can drown myself and never have to relive this embarrassment.

"Where are you going?" Louie asks when I tug my arm free from his grasp.

"Swimming," I tell him.

"You're not swimming, Charlotte. You're drunk," he says, his heavy footsteps right behind me.

Why does the sound of my name coming out of his mouth send shivers down my spine?

"That's why we came up here. You promised." I turn around and give him my best pout.

"I didn't promise. And you can swim when you're not drunk," he tells me.

"Well, it's a good thing you're not my dad, or my boyfriend, or my fiancé, or... Well, the point is, you can't tell me what I can and can't do. And right now,

I'm jumping in that pool." Sliding the door open, I get one step outside before I feel Louie's arm wrap around my waist and pull me back up against his chest.

"No, you're not. You'll drown," he says.

I shrug a shoulder. "It's not like anyone would miss me," I tell him, shaking out of his hold. I lift my top over my head, not caring that I don't have a bra on.

"Fuck," Louie hisses.

My shorts are next. They flutter to the ground as I eye Louie over a shoulder. "I guess if you don't want me to drown, you're going to have to come in with me." I smile at him and then jump into the water.

"Are you fucking serious? Get out of the pool, Charlotte," Louie growls.

"Make me." I cup some water in my hand and splash it in his direction. "Oh, look, you're wet now. You might as well get in."

Louie stares at me as he silently removes his jacket, then his tie and his shirt.

Holy mother of god, I did not think this through clearly. What on earth have I done?

Louie toes off his shoes, and then bends down and

grabs his socks. When his hands land on his belt, I swallow. This is too much. *He* is too much. That chest, those abs. I've only ever seen pictures of men like him in Calvin Klein ads. His arms and chest are covered in black-and-white tattoos. Intricate lines and curves. I'm frozen to the spot. Thankfully, my feet can touch the bottom, otherwise I would have sunk for sure.

Louie is down to a pair of black boxer briefs that do nothing to hide the outline of his cock. *That can't be real. It's huge.* Then he lowers himself to the edge of the pool and slides in. I don't move as he makes his way towards me.

"You should have gotten out, Charlotte," he says in a low growl.

"Why?" I ask him.

"Because now I have you practically naked in front of me," he says. He hasn't reached out to touch me, and I do nothing to cover my naked breasts from his view.

"What are you going to do to me?"

"What do you want me to do?" Louie takes a step closer.

What do I want him to do? I can still feel the effects of the alcohol. There is no way I'd be naked in front of him if I were completely sober. There are a lot of things I wouldn't do if I weren't a little tipsy. "I want you to show me," I tell him.

"Show you what?"

"Show me how you'd shatter my entire world," I whisper. I can't believe I'm asking a stranger to give me an orgasm. This isn't me. I've never had a one-night stand before. But this is Vegas. What happens in Vegas and all that.

"You're drunk." Louie's eyes darken as he hooks an arm around my waist.

"Not that drunk." My legs wrap around his hips at the same time my arms hook over his neck. "Make me forget," I plead with him, silently praying he doesn't turn me down.

"You'll regret this when you sober up," he says.

"I won't. Unless you can't put your money where your mouth is. You could just be all talk." I doubt it, but I don't know him. He might be a dud in the bedroom.

The corners of his lips tilt up. "You really want this?"

I nod a little too enthusiastically. "I really want this." *And I do.*

"You were engaged to another man just two days ago, Charlotte," Louie reminds me.

"I was going to his room to call off the wedding.

I'd already decided I couldn't go through with it. I'm not sad because my fiancé cheated on me," I explain.

Louie's fingertips run down my cheek. "Then why are you sad?"

"Because he stole my sister from me," I say. "I only have one of those. I can't replace her." I take a deep breath. "And I've spent the last two years of my life having mediocre sex and faking orgasms. I want good sex."

Louie smiles. "That's a long time to tolerate bad sex." He walks towards the edge of the pool. My back presses against the cold tiles and his cock presses against my core, lighting up something I thought was long dead inside me.

"Please," I beg.

"*Please* what?" Louie asks, brushing his cock against my core again.

"Shatter my entire world." My voice is quiet, almost a whisper.

"Remember, you asked for it," Louie tells me, and then I'm being lifted out of the water. My butt lands on the edge of the pool. "Lie back."

I do what he says without hesitation, and then his fingers are hooking into the sides of my panties.

"I'm not asking again, Charlotte. You want me to rock your world? I'm going to rock you into another atmosphere." He drags the fabric down my legs before tossing it to the side of the pool. Louie's hands land on each side of my thighs, and my legs slowly spread open. "Mine," he says before I feel his tongue on my most sensitive parts.

My thighs try to close. I don't know why, but this is more intimate than I thought this would be. Owen never went down on me. He didn't like it.

"Keep them open," Louie grunts as his tongue slides up. His mouth closes around my clit and then he sucks.

"Oh god." My hands ball into fists at my sides. "Shit!" I scream out as he holds my legs open, his fingers digging into my upper thighs.

Louie isn't just going down on me. He's eating me out like I'm his last meal. And holy freaking shit, my stomach tightens. I can feel the cress of an orgasm building.

"Don't stop!" I cry out.

"I'm not stopping," Louie says, and continues to lick, suck, and nibble on me. Within seconds, I'm flying over the edge into the abyss. My entire body shakes with the orgasm that tears through me.

When this man said he'd shatter my world, he wasn't lying.

Chapter Seven

Louie

I'm no stranger to seeing a woman come apart underneath me. But this? Charlotte letting go and screaming in ecstasy... It's something else. I've never been as hard for anyone as I am for her right now. I don't just want to slam my cock into her warm heat. *I need to*. More than I need air.

I climb out of the pool and pick up her limp

body. "That was just the appetizer. We've still got the main course and dessert to go, babe," I tell her before walking into the penthouse, towards the main bedroom.

"That was an appetizer?" Charlotte asks, her head resting on my shoulder. "What's the main course?"

I can't stop the laugh bubbling in my chest. "You'll see," I say as I toss her onto the bed.

"Ah, shit, we're going to get the sheets all wet!" she squeals.

"In more ways than one, I hope." I slide my boxers down to my ankles and step out of them. When I straighten back up, Charlotte is leaning on her elbows. Her eyes are wide, her mouth hangs open, and she's staring at my cock. My fist wraps around the base before giving it a slight tug.

"Wh... what is that?" she asks, not taking her eyes off my dick.

"This is what's going to make you scream so much your throat is going to hurt tomorrow," I tell her.

"That... Does it hurt?" Her shocked expression morphs into curiosity.

"Are you a virgin?" I don't care either way. I need to sink into her. Doesn't matter if there are barriers I have to break through. Nothing is stopping me from feeling her cunt wrapped around my cock.

"No. Does it hurt?" she asks again.

"No. And I promise these are here for your pleasure." My thumb runs down the multiple piercings that line my shaft.

"What's that called? There's a name for it, right?"

"A Jacob's ladder," I explain. My hands land on her thighs, spreading them open before I climb onto the bed. "Tell me you want this, Charlotte. Tell me you want me to fuck you into oblivion. Tell me you want me to make you feel like no one else has ever made you feel before." The tips of my fingers slide through her wet folds, and her body shutters beneath my touch.

"I want that. All of that," she says, falling back onto the bed.

My fingers glide into her opening. I scissor them inside her, trying to warm her up. She's fucking tight. I told her it wouldn't hurt. But, fuck, it just might.

"You're so fucking tight." I lean forward, and my mouth latches on to one of her breasts. Sucking and nibbling on her nipple.

"S... s... sorry," Charlotte says, her back arching off the bed.

"Don't be. I'll go slow. I want you to enjoy every second of this." I remove my fingers, line my cock up with her entrance, and slowly push in. Charlotte's body stiffens. Her fingernails dig into my arms. "Relax. I need you to let me in."

"It's too big. I know that sounds stupid and cliché, but that thing is not fitting inside me, Louie," she says, shaking her head.

I slide in another inch and pull out before sliding in a little farther again. My thumb circles her clit. "It's going to fit, and it's going to fit perfectly. Your pussy was made for me. Look how good you're doing, taking everything I'm giving you." I push up on an arm and look at where our bodies are joined. "Fuck, that's hot."

"It feels so... different..."

"Different good or different bad?" I ask, pausing my movements.

"Good. Definitely good," Charlotte says quickly, and I start moving in and out of her again. Slowly.

She's not wrong. It does feel different. I've never felt a pussy like this before. It's never felt this good. Then I stare down at my cock and realize why. I forgot a condom. I'm not about to stop now, though. *Fuck that.* I'll pull out. It'll be fine.

I'm almost all the way in. With one last thrust, I

bury myself to the hilt in her cunt. Charlotte cries out. My body falls over hers, and her arms wrap around my neck, pulling me closer to her.

Her lips press against mine. I pause momentarily, until her tongue pushes through the seam of my mouth and I cave. I'm not a kisser. But I'm also not going to deny this woman something so simple. My hips start thrusting in and out of her, picking up speed, as our tongues duel.

Charlotte moans into my mouth, her legs wrap around my waist, and her hips start moving in time with my thrusts. "Don't stop," she says, breaking away from the kiss.

"I'm not stopping until I feel you come all over my dick," I tell her. Driving in harder, faster.

"Oh... yes!" she screams, her nails scratching into the side of my neck. Her pussy tightens around my cock, squeezing so fucking hard I think she might actually break me in half.

Pulling out, I fist my cock and pump a few times before I'm spilling my seed all over her stomach. "So fucking hot." Then I lean forward and capture her lips.

Now I'm kissing her? What is this woman doing to me?

"Mmm, what's for dessert?" Charlotte asks.

73

"Give me a couple of minutes, and we can dive right into dessert," I tell her, falling next to her on the bed. I wrap an arm around her waist and pull her body on top of mine. "Fuck, you're gorgeous." My hands move her wet hair away from her face. "I've never seen anything more beautiful."

"You've already got me in your bed. You can lose the lines," she says, trying to squirm her way off me.

I tighten my hold on her back and look her dead in the eye. "They're not lines. I don't waste my time saying shit I don't mean, Charlotte."

She stares blankly at me, blinking a few times before she closes her eyes. "Am I bad at sex?"

"Why the fuck would you think you're bad at sex?" I ask her. "Open your eyes and look at me."

Her lashes flutter before she meets my glare. That's when I notice tears forming. "Just tell me the truth. Am I bad?"

"Fuck no. You couldn't be bad at it even if you tried," I tell her. "Being inside you is like nothing I've ever felt. It's amazing. Don't ever doubt yourself." My lips press against her forehead. "We should have a bath."

"A bath? Why?"

"Because that's where dessert is being served." I roll over before standing and picking her up.

"I can walk," she protests, trying to wiggle out of my hold again.

"You can, but I can also carry you. And having your naked body pressed up against mine isn't a hardship." In fact, I'm pretty certain I could get used to it.

Chapter Eight

My head is pounding, and my body aches as if I've run a thousand miles. Flashes of what I did come back to me before I even open my eyes. Maybe if I don't move, it won't be real? These soft sheets I'm feeling against my skin—my naked skin—aren't real.

Shit... My *naked* skin.

My eyes snap open, scanning the room, and I breathe a sigh of relief when I don't find anyone else in here with me. I'm alone. It was a dream, right? Except this isn't the room I was staying in. This is the same room from my dream.

"Oh my god!" I pull the blanket up over my face. It wasn't a dream. It was real. He was real. How? The things that man did to me, his body, his... dick. No way that was real. Nothing that good can be real.

The visions running through my mind are very real, though. And oh my gosh, I never in my wildest dreams would have thought I'd be capable of having a moment—no, not a moment. Hours and hours of such... passion.

Louie. I say his name in my head. It's not like I didn't scream it out enough. I vaguely remember him saying my throat would be sore. And sure enough, when I swallow, it hurts. I need water. I need to get the hell out of Dodge before this empty room becomes *not so empty*.

I should be mortified I'm waking up alone, but I'm not. I'm relieved. No awkward morning after. Or in this case, *night* after. When I look out the windows, the city lights flash against the darkened sky.

Every muscle hurts as I drag myself out of bed.

Who needs to go to a gym for a workout? Just spend a few hours naked with Louie.

Huh, I wonder why no one has marketed sex as a weight loss solution yet? Probably because sex isn't normally like that, at least not in my experience.

I find my clothes neatly folded on a chair by the window. Who folds someone else's clothes? Psychopaths, that's who. Great, I had sex with a damn psycho. At least he left my body in one piece, and I'm not currently in a shallow grave in the Nevada desert somewhere. Thank god for small miracles.

Then again, if I were dead right now, Owen and my sister would blame themselves and have to live with the guilt. Guess there is always a bright side to messed-up situations. Not that I'm planning on dying. I guess not many people plan on being cut to pieces by a psycho, though.

I grab my pile of clothes and set them down on the bed. My top and shorts are here, but my underwear is nowhere to be found. Then I remember... Louie took them off me by the pool. I slide my shorts up my legs, pull my top on over my head, and quickly run into the bathroom to freshen up the best I can without a toothbrush or a comb. Then, tiptoeing out of the bedroom, I scan the small hallway before I walk down. I can't hear a single sound. I must be alone in the penthouse.

I make my way towards the glass doors that lead out to the pool and gently slide them open. I don't want to make any noise just in case Louie is lurking around here somewhere. I'd prefer not to see him right now. I look around the edge of the pool for my underwear, but there's nothing. Great, some poor cleaning lady is probably going to find my panties in the most random place. Mission *unaccomplished*, I walk back through the doors and get halfway across the small living room before I'm stopped by a man. A huge bulking monster of a man.

"Running out?" Sammie says. I remember him from last night. He's one of Louie's friends.

Oh god, please tell me this isn't one of those situations where friends share or *think* they can share me. I might have been explorative with Louie today, but that's where my spice level ends.

"Ah... I was just leaving," I say, trying to sound confident in my response.

"You should probably put shoes on first. The streets out there are filthy," Sammie tells me.

"Right." I look around. *Where did I leave my shoes?*

"They're by the door. Boss said to wait here until you woke up. He didn't want you waking up alone."

"Boss?" I parrot.

"Louie," Sammie clarifies.

"Why do you call him *boss*?" I ask as I try skirting around the man and front of me to make my way towards the door.

"Because he is the boss. Where are you running off to anyway?"

"The closest health clinic," I blurt out. Shit. Some thoughts are supposed to stay inside my head. That's a problem I seem to be having more and more, though. I know how irresponsible I was with Louie, which is why the first stop I'm gonna make when I leave this room is a clinic.

Sammie's eyes widen and then a weird, worried expression crosses his features. "Shit, are you sick? I can have the doc come up and check you out," he says while retrieving his phone.

"I'm not sick. At least I hope not. It's... personal. I just... Anyway, tell Louie I said thanks—or don't tell him that. I'm just gonna go." I open the door, walk over to the elevators, and quickly press the button.

Sammie follows me. "I'll take you," he says.

"Excuse me?"

"I'll take you to the clinic. Which one do you want to go to?" he asks me.

"I can take myself." I have absolutely no intention of having one of Louie's friends... employees... whatever... take me to a sexual health clinic. Could life get any more embarrassing?

"Look, if you don't let me take you I'm going to get fired, or worse. So *please* just let me drive you to wherever you gotta go," he pleads.

"You're not going to get fired. Tell your boss I refused your assistance." I shrug and step into the elevator when the doors open, only to have Sammie follow me again.

"Yeah, you don't know the boss too well. Trust me when I say it's in my best interest to take you." Sammie smiles at me. It's awkward—although I think he's going for *charming*.

"You're right. I don't know your boss, which is exactly why I need to go to a clinic to get tested for everything and anything after spending hours and hours having unprotected sex with him. So if you don't mind, it's not exactly something I'm proud of. And, honestly, I don't need an audience with a front-row seat to my embarrassment." I don't know why I have no filter at the moment. Lingering effects of alcohol maybe? Or I'm just tired and emotionally drained.

I can see Sammie's lips twitch, as if he's trying his damnedest not to smile or laugh. And he better not, because right now, I feel violent. I know I can't take him, but I'd go down giving it my best.

"Unprotected? You sure?" he asks with furrowed brows.

I blink at him. *Is he seriously asking me that?* "Oh, great, he has some horrible sexually transmitted disease, doesn't he? And I was thinking the worst that could happen was he'd be a psycho and cut my body up into tiny pieces."

"You might be closer on the psycho theory. Pretty sure boss is clean, though. No STDs I know of. I also doubt very much he'd cut your body up into tiny pieces." Sammie laughs. The asshole actually laughs.

"Still, I think I'll go to a clinic and make sure." The doors finally open and I step out. It takes me a hot minute to orientate myself and find the sign that reads *rideshare*. I try to ignore that Sammie is still following me and that people seem to be making a path when I walk by.

Do they all know? Is it written on my face? The

fact that I probably contracted an STD that's going to be my undoing? That would be my luck. Have the best sex of my life, only for it to be the thing that kills me.

Grabbing my phone, which was thankfully still in the back pocket of my shorts, I call for an Uber. "You really don't need to follow me," I tell Sammie.

"I really do," he says as he types something into his phone.

"My ride is two minutes away. I'm fine, honestly," I assure him.

"Mmhmm," he groans, still staring at his screen.

When the car pulls up, Sammie beats me to the handle, holding the door open for me. "Thanks." I frown at him.

Why is he so insistent? At least now that the car's here, I can finally be alone—well, besides the driver. My hopes are immediately demolished when Sammie climbs into the back seat with me.

"What are you doing?" I ask him.

"I told you. Going with you," he says. "I happen to value my life, which is why I'm not taking any chances."

"I can text you or something, if I find out your boss has a disease you need to know about."

The guy in the driver's seat chokes as he stares at us in the rearview mirror. "Drive. And pretend you didn't hear a word in this car," Sammie tells him in a much firmer tone than I've ever heard him use on me.

"Yes, sir." The man's face pales as he pulls out into traffic.

Hey, world, if ever there was a time for a sinkhole to appear, now would be it.

"Does Nevada have sinkholes?" I ask Sammie.

"Some parts, but not the part you're in. Why?" he replies.

"Pity," I groan and lean my head back on the seat before closing my eyes.

Chapter Nine

I can't believe I left a beautiful woman in bed to deal with this shit. And not just any beautiful woman either. Charlotte. Her face is painted in my memory. I might have spent an hour watching her sleep, cataloguing every single one of her features.

I've always been able to find flaws in people. But

no matter how hard I look, I can't find a single fucking flaw on that woman.

Her screams replay like a song in my mind. I was prepared to wait for her to wake up and take her again. It seems the world chose tonight to fuck up my plans. Or rather, the dipshit currently tied to a wooden chair in front of me did.

My right fist swings out, connecting with his jaw. His head snaps to the side and blood splatters from his mouth. Am I enjoying hitting him? *Fuck yes, I am.* It's because of him I'm not currently in bed with Charlotte. Then, there's the fact he was dumb enough to betray me...

"Did you really think I wouldn't find you?"

"I didn't..." His voice breaks off when my fist connects with his jaw again.

This asshole thought he could dish out details of our operation to some lowlife thug who decided he'd try to take what was mine. It wasn't the first time and I know it won't be the last either. When you're at the top of the food chain, everyone wants what's rightfully yours.

The idiot who paid for intel from the soon-to-be dead man in my chair was caught red-handed. "You didn't what? Think I'd find out?" I ask. I turn around and walk over to the opposite side of the room. Carlo is watching with a smirk on his face. He knows what's coming.

I could end this right here and now, but where would the fun be in that? Any fucker who betrays me doesn't get the mercy of a quick, painless death.

"Please, Louie, I didn't know what he was gonna do. I needed the money. My ma needs surgery," the fucker cries out.

"If you needed money, you should have asked me for more work instead of stealing from me," I say, knowing full well this cocksucker doesn't have a mother.

I have files on every single member of my organization. I don't let anyone come onboard without a thorough background check. And this guy? Justin? He has no family. Grew up in the system, thrown out onto the streets at eighteen.

Picking up the metal branding pole, I walk over to the fire and hold the end over the flames. The flat side is in the shape of a playing card with the word "renegade" carved out in the middle of it. Anyone who goes against the laws I've laid down in this city gets branded. It shows everyone else what happens when they try to go against me.

I'll make sure this asshole's body is found—every now and then, you have to make an example.

"You see, you're going to help others not make the same mistake you have, Justin." I watch the metal heat up until it's glowing red. "When they see this brand on you, they'll think twice about betraying me."

Once I'm satisfied that the metal is hot enough to do its job, I slowly walk over to a now-screaming Justin. He's struggling against his restraints. I lift a foot and kick him square in the chest, knocking him and the chair over so he's laid out flat on his back. I hold him still with my foot while I bring the brand down right in the center of his torso. The smell of burned flesh assaults me. Justin's screams die off, and his body stops moving.

"He passed out. Didn't take long." Carlo walks over, peering down at Justin before looking up at me again. "You might want to check your phone, boss. Sammie is trying to reach you."

I pause. The metal rod drops next to Justin's head, landing on the concrete floor with a clank. I left Sammie with Charlotte. I didn't want her to wake up alone and think I skipped out on her.

I quickly pull out my phone and find three messages.

SAMMIE:

> Boss, your girl wants to go to a
> health clinic. Something about
> unprotected sex?

SAMMIE:

> Unprotected? Really, have you lost
> your goddamn mind?

SAMMIE:

> In a car with her now. She offered
> to let me know if you have any
> STDs, btw.

What the actual fuck?

I hit dial on his number, and Sammie answers after two rings. "Boss."

"Where the fuck is she?" I grunt. *And why does she think she needs to go to a clinic? Is she sick?*

"Right next to me. Wanna talk to her?" Sammie says, humor evident in his tone.

"Yes."

"Hello?" A sweet southern voice fills my ears.

"Charlotte, are you okay? Are you ill?" I ask her.

"No, I'm not *ill*," she says.

"Then why are you going to a clinic?"

"Because we... well, you know. And I don't know what kind of diseases you may or may not have," she whispers into the phone.

"I'm clean," I tell her.

"Thanks, but I think I'll stick with the medical tests." She sighs. "Look, I had fun. It *was* fun, but you can tell your guard dog here to leave me alone now."

"Give the phone back to Sammie." I'm not mad that she wants to go and get checked out after having unprotected sex. It's smart on her part. It's not something she should be doing alone, though.

"Boss?" Sammie asks.

"Stay with her. Text me the address and I'll meet you there." I cut the call and walk over to the sink, strip out of my shirt, and wash my hands. The water turns red with the fucker's blood. "Finish up here. I've got something to do," I call out to Carlo.

"Yeah, you know what's worse than an STD? A kid. Unprotected? That's not like you," he replies.

"How the fuck would you know how I fuck?" I lift a questioning brow in his direction.

"I don't. But you're smart, and not wrapping it isn't smart." He shrugs.

I don't care what these fuckers think. Was it smart? *No.* Do I regret it? *Also, no.* Being inside Charlotte is probably the best thing I've ever felt. And it's something I plan on feeling again as soon as possible.

I pull into the parking lot at the health clinic a few minutes after Sammie sent me the details. And when I walk inside, I find Charlotte sitting in the waiting area. The moment Sammie spots me, he stands and walks over.

"You want me to stick around?" he asks.

"Nah, I got it. Go help Carlo," I tell him.

"Gladly." Sammie smiles. I guess disposing of a body is better than sitting in a health clinic. At least for him it is. Right now, there is no place I would rather be than here, supporting this woman.

I take the chair my friend just vacated, and Charlotte looks over at me. "You didn't need to come here."

"You should have waited for me. I would have called the doc in for whatever tests you wanted," I tell her.

Charlotte blinks at me. "Why are you here?"

"Because you're here." I shrug.

"Don't you have things to do?" she asks.

"What's more important than making sure neither of us has any diseases?" I counter. "If you're going to get tested, it's only right that I do it with you."

"Yeah? You going to ask them to give you the morning-after pill too?" She raises a challenging brow.

"The what now?" I know what the morning-after pill is. I just don't agree with her taking one. Something about it doesn't sit right with me.

"The morning-after pill. It's this magic little pill that will hopefully ensure I don't end up pregnant," she explains.

"You don't want kids?"

"I do, actually. But I'd prefer to be married to their father first. Being a single mom may not be totally avoidable—because who knows? I could end up marrying some deadbeat asshole. That said, it's not something I'm gonna set out to do," she says.

"Don't take the pill," I tell her, and Charlotte's head whips in my direction.

"Excuse me?"

"Look, I get it. Your body, your choice. And I'm one hundred percent onboard with that. But, if you're only taking the pill because you think you'll be a single mom with a deadbeat for a baby daddy, then I'll be the first to tell you that's not happening here. I wouldn't abandon you or any child I helped create."

Charlotte shakes her head. "You don't even know me."

"I know enough." I lean in closer to her. "I know how you taste. I know how you sound when you come, and I know the way your brows crease when an orgasm hits you. I know that you talk in your sleep, and I know that you're smart. Probably too smart to be mixed up with the likes of me."

"Oh god, what did I say in my sleep?" she gasps.

"That's what you took from all that?" I smile at her. I swear this woman is never what I expect.

"Well, no, but seriously whatever I said, I was asleep and it can't be held against me." She looks away as her cheeks turn a deeper shade of pink.

"Don't worry. You didn't say anything bad. Just that I was the best sex of your life and that you couldn't wait to do it again." I smirk.

"I did not say that." She turns back in my direction.

"No, you didn't, but am I wrong?" I raise a brow at her, and she shakes her head. Little does she know, as soon as we're done here, I plan on taking her back to my place and not letting her out of bed for at least a week.

Chapter Ten

Charlotte

My head is spinning. This cannot be my life right now. How is this happening? I'm sitting in a health clinic with the man who, just hours ago, was screwing my brains out. This isn't me. I'm not the girl who has one-night stands or one-day stands or what-ever this is. I'm also not the girl who's considering

97

listening to a complete stranger when he tells me I don't need the morning-after pill.

"If it makes you feel any better, I pulled out every time," he says, his voice low enough that only I can hear it.

I can feel my face heat up. "It doesn't," I tell him.

"Miss Armstrong." A man in a white doctor's coat calls out for me.

I stand and take in a huge breath of air. It's no big deal. Lots of people do this. I think. I'm not the first, and I'm sure I won't be the last person to come into this clinic after having irresponsible sex. Great sex, but I don't think the doctor cares too much about Louie's performance level.

Louie stands with me. His hand lands on my lower back, and I still. "What are you doing?" I ask him.

"Coming with you," he says with his brows drawn together. "You're not going back there with some guy you don't even know."

"Oh, like I went up to that penthouse with you?" I ask him. "And it's not some guy. It's a doctor."

"We did this together, which means we're doing this part together too." Louie presses on my lower back, urging me to continue walking.

"I really don't think you need to come in with

me. You can make your own separate appointment," I tell him.

Louie smirks. "I disagree. I think I very much need to come in with you."

"Is there a problem, Miss Armstrong?" the doctor asks.

"No," Louie answers before I can, only to hold out a hand to introduce himself. "Sorry, Doc, Louie Giuliani."

"Mr. Giuliani, welcome. Come on back, sir," the doctor says, his posture stiff and his face a little pale as he holds the door open for us.

I look from the doctor to Louie. *What the hell? I* know he claims to own a casino but why does it seem as if he's more important than that?

Louie doesn't move his hand the entire way as we enter the doctor's office. He sits next to me and then picks up my palm. "We're here for testing. Every STD you can think of."

Oh my god, kill me now. "Just the standard tests you'd run after someone has unprotected sex with a stranger will be fine. And a script for the morning-after pill," I clarify.

I feel Louie's hand tighten around mine with that last part. I ignore him and keep my gaze focused on the doctor, who looks to Louie for... something. What? I have no idea.

"Whatever she wants," Louie tells him.

"Okay. I'll need you to change into a gown and hop up on the bed for me, Miss Armstrong," the doctor says.

"Why?" Louie asks.

"So I can perform an exam."

"Absolutely fucking not," Louie growls. "Can't you just do blood tests?"

"Okay. Sure." The doctor quickly agrees with a nod, and I interject.

"Wait... What tests will I miss if you don't do a physical exam?"

The doctor clears his throat and swallows before responding. "It's not necessary unless you are experiencing unusual discharge or anything else out of the ordinary."

"She's not," Louie says.

"I have a voice," I tell him.

"And I know your vagina is fucking perfect. There's nothing wrong with it," he grunts.

My eyes widen. I think he's trying to kill me from embarrassment. "Oh my god!" I hiss at him, then turn back to the doctor. "I'm so sorry. Let's do the blood test and the pill please."

"What's wrong?" Louie asks. After the clinic, he ushered me into his car. He then stopped at a drug store, plucked the script from my hands, and went in to get me that little magic pill I wanted.

The thing is, now that I have it, I'm not sure I want to take it anymore. I know I'm not likely to get pregnant from our time together, especially because he's so sure of the fact that he pulled out. It's not that, though. I've always wanted kids, just not with a stranger.

I mean, what would I tell my child? *Sorry you don't have a dad. I got knocked up when I ran away to Vegas this one time.*

"I'm not sure." I sigh. "This is just... not me."

"What's not you?" Louie presses.

"The one-night stand, the morning-after pill, Vegas... All of this isn't me." I shake my head. I don't think I'm explaining myself very well.

"What if it's not a one-night stand?" he asks me.

"What?"

"What if this thing with us doesn't stop after

today? What if it goes into tomorrow and the next day?"

"I just left my fiancé at the altar. I don't think I should be jumping into any kind of relationship so soon."

"You left a cheating bastard who didn't deserve you, Charlotte, and there is no timeframe for you to start living your life for you. You must have dreams. There has to be something you wanted to do?" Louie says as he pulls out into traffic.

What do I want to do? I thought I knew. I thought I wanted to be married. I thought I was ready for the white-picket fence. It just wasn't with Owen. I knew that *before* I caught him in bed with my sister.

"I don't know what I want," I admit aloud.

"You wanna know a secret?" Louie asks me.

"What?"

"You don't need to know. You can take as much time as you need to figure out what you want to do next."

"I have to go home and face reality eventually." I can't afford to stay in Vegas.

"You have your penthouse room at the Royal Flush for as long as you want it," Louie says, as if reading my mind.

"It was you, wasn't it? I didn't win anything, did I?" I knew it was too good to be true.

"You won my attention. It's debatable whether or not that's a good thing." The corner of his lips tip up.

From my experience, this man's attention has been a very good thing—*orgasmic even*.

Chapter Eleven

I get all the way back to the penthouse floor with Charlotte. She looks a little lost. I get that I'm probably coming off too strong. I can't help it. I see something I want and I go after it with everything I have. And right now, the thing I want is her.

kylie Kent

Charlotte will either get onboard with the program or she'll get onboard with the program. Because I don't give up. Nothing is going to stop me from having her. Completely. I don't know when it happened. But sometime between leaving her in that bed asleep and the doctor's visit, I made up my mind.

This woman is mine.

I was going to take her to my penthouse. Instead, I lead her towards the room she's staying in. It's a small compromise on my part. To make her feel more comfortable. "Thank you for bringing me back," she says.

"Of course. Do you need anything? Are you hungry?" I ask as I walk farther into the suite.

"Ah, no. I'm good. Thanks." Charlotte's fingers twirl in her shirt.

I open my mouth to say something to ease her mind, and then my phone rings. It's Sammie. *Shit.* "I'm sorry. I have to take this."

"It's okay. I'm going to have a shower. Thanks for... everything." Charlotte turns towards the bedroom.

"Charlotte?"

"Yeah?" She stops and pivots to look at me again.

"This isn't over. I'll be back," I tell her.

106

"You don't have to."

"I want to," I say and click the button to answer my phone. "This better be important," I grunt as I walk out of the penthouse and back towards the bank of elevators.

"Some detective is downstairs hassling the staff. He's looking for your girl," Sammie says.

"I'll be right down," I tell him before cutting the call.

I was wondering how long it'd take for Charlotte's ex to come looking for her. He was quicker than I thought. My guess was at least a week. My staff knows not to say shit about any of our guests. Which means, badge or not, the guy ain't getting any information out of them.

By the time I make it down to reception, I can hear the commotion. "Is there a problem here?" I ask.

Sammie is behind the check-in desk, standing in front of a young girl who looks like she's about ready to cry. My friend, however, appears as though *he's ready* to jump over the counter and end this motherfucker in front of everyone.

Interesting. He's usually the most easygoing out of the three of us.

"Yeah, I want to speak to the manager," Charlotte's dipshit ex says. *Owen*, if my memory serves me right. And I'm always right.

"And you are?" I ask him.

"Detective Aiken. I'm looking for a woman who checked into this hotel two days ago," he says, flashing a badge.

I shove my hands into my pockets and pin him with a glare. "You got a warrant?"

"Do I need one?" he counters.

"Yes. We don't give out guest information unless you have a warrant," I tell him.

"Look, she's my fiancée. She went missing. I'm just trying to find the woman I'm supposed to be marrying, and I know she was here. Just tell me if she's still here," he pleads.

I smirk. "Again, get a warrant. Until then, get out of my casino. And if I catch you back around here harassing my staff, I will press charges. I don't give a fuck what kind of badge you try flashing in my direction." I know he's not going to get the paperwork he needs. No judge in this city will sign off on searching one of my casinos. I nod my head at the two security guys. "Escort Mr. Aikens out and don't let him back in unless he has a warrant."

"Yes, boss."

Then I turn back to the girl manning the front desk. "Did you tell him she was here?"

"No," she whispers while shaking her head.

"Good." I need to get back upstairs. But first I need to have a chat with my friends. "Get Carlo. Meet me in my office," I tell Sammie.

"So you shacked up with a runaway bride?" Sammie laughs.

"Fuck off," I grunt at him before downing the contents of my whiskey glass.

"So this detective, he cheated on her? Fucking fool." Carlo whistles. "Girl's a solid ten."

I raise a brow at him. I'm not opposed to putting a bullet between his eyes if he's looking at Charlotte the wrong kind of way. Like I said, I will stop at nothing to get what I want and keep it.

"Objectively speaking," he adds, holding up his hands. "Trust me, boss, she's all yours."

"That's if you can keep her. She's smart, that one," Sammie chimes in.

"You think I can't keep her?" I ask, genuinely

curious as to why the fuck he thinks I won't be able to keep her.

"Does she know who you are?" he counters. "She's a good girl type. Doesn't fit in with our world."

"She fits in if I say she does," I tell him before changing the subject. "How'd it go with Justin?"

"Splayed him out. I'm expecting it to hit the media anytime now. Left him in an alleyway behind one of the Garcia restaurants," Carlo says.

The Garcias are pains in my ass. Their empire is building, not as large as mine, but they're giving it their best shot.

"Get anything else out of him?" I know there was a reason Justin sold insider intel, and it sure as fuck wasn't for a sick mother who doesn't exist.

"Nope. But I have my suspicions. I've got a few guys hitting the streets tonight. Once they find him, people will start talking and our guys will be there to hear 'em."

"Good. Keep me posted. I got shit to do." By this time, I'm usually walking the floor, mingling with high rollers and making my presence known. Right now, all I want to do is get back upstairs to Charlotte.

I hear it as soon as I open the penthouse door. Her cries. I run through the living room and find

Charlotte curled up on the bed. Sobbing. The sound —the image of her so upset—has my chest aching.

"Charlotte? What happened?" I ask as I climb onto the bed and pick her up. I sit her on my lap and hold her against my chest. Her sobs get harder, louder, and my hands are ready to get stained with the blood of whoever the fuck made this woman cry.

Chapter Twelve

T he moment Louie's arms wrap around me, I lose any control I thought I might have had. My cries turn into full-blown sobs. My tears stain his shirt. I'm a mess. I don't know what happened. After he left, I swallowed that pill, had a shower, put a robe on, and sat on the bed. Then the next thing I knew, I was crying.

"What happened?" Louie asks again, his fingers stroking my hair.

"My life is a mess," I manage to get out through heaves. I'm trying to stop. I shouldn't be seeking comfort from a stranger.

"Is it a mess or is it just beginning?" Louie asks.

"What do you mean?" I push myself off him, sitting cross-legged on the bed. I use the sleeve of the robe to wipe at my face. Disgusting as it is, it's all I have.

"I mean, what if your life isn't a mess? This could be the best thing that ever happened to you, Charlotte. You get a fresh start. A chance to recreate yourself to the version of you that you want to be. Not the version that others want you to be."

Is he right? Have I spent my whole life pretending to be one thing when I'm really another? I don't think I have. I like myself. I liked my life... mostly.

"I was ready to call off my wedding. I don't know why, but I knew I didn't love him enough to marry him."

"That took a lot of guts for you to do that," Louie tells me.

"But instead of breaking up with Owen, I found him fucking my sister and I ran."

"I'm not going to lie. I'm glad you ran here. That

I met you. I'm glad that you're here." Louie takes hold of my hands.

"Thank you," I whisper. "I'm sorry."

"For what?" His brows furrow.

"For crying on you. I ruined your shirt. You don't even know me and you're sitting in here comforting me."

"I don't know you yet. But do *you* know you, Charlotte?" Louie asks.

"I thought I did," I admit.

"I want you to take your time. Really think about what you want from life. And while you're doing that, I think it'd be a great idea for us to get to know each other," he says.

I smile. I like this man. He is absolutely nothing like anyone I know. "Yeah, like dating? Or friends? Or..." I let my sentence trail off.

"Dating. We should definitely date," Louie says. "In fact, the first date starts right now." He stands and holds out a hand to me. "Come on."

"Wait! Now? Where? I'm not dressed." My eyes widen. *Is he insane?* I can't go out right now. I'm a hot mess. I don't even need a mirror to confirm that.

"I like you in a state of undress." Louie smirks. "And you don't need to change for where we're

115

going. Trust me." He's still holding out his hand, waiting for me to take it.

Why do I feel like this is one of those moments? A crossroad in my life? A red pill, blue pill type of thing. I can stay here and wallow in my own self-pity, or I can take Louie's hand and turn my life around.

It could be a turn for the better or for the worse, but there's only one way to find out, right?

I place my palm in his. "Okay, but I'm not walking through the casino in a robe."

"I wouldn't let you walk anywhere in public without clothes," Louie says as he leads me out of the room.

We end up in front of a door in the same corridor. Louie opens it and guides me inside. It's similar to the room we just left. But less *hotel* and more *lived-in*.

"Do you live here?" I ask him.

"I do." He nods once before adding, "Make yourself at home. I'll be right back." And then he's disappearing down a hall.

Make myself at home, huh? Does that mean I get snooping privileges? I mean, it would only be smart to look around, right? Try to figure out who this guy is that I'm... dating?

Though I'm not so sure dating is a wise thing for

me to do. I also don't think I want to refuse him. Like I said, I've never met anyone like Louie. And right now, I really, really am interested in getting to know him better. Him and that body of his.

Oh shit, I've been single for a hot minute and I've turned into a hussy. Or is it the fact that he rocked my entire world with orgasms that I didn't know I was capable of having? Either way, I want more.

Chapter Thirteen

I leave Charlotte in the living area. After placing an order for room service, I rush around the bedroom. I remove the pistol from under the pillow on the bed. The one hidden behind the cushion on the sofa, and then I walk into the bathroom and grab the one that's taped to the side of the toilet.

Sounds paranoid, but I'd rather be paranoid than caught off guard and out of reach of a weapon.

Next I walk into the closet, unlock the safe, and stow everything away in there. Before rushing back out to the living room, because I know there are more lying around. Most of them not in obvious places, though. She wouldn't find them. Unless...

"Charlotte?" I question when I find her staring into a drawer I really wish she hadn't opened.

"Shit. Sorry. I was totally snooping. But in my defense, you left me alone out here," she says, slamming the drawer shut again.

"Snoop away," I say, holding my hands up as if I've got nothing to hide. Other than a few weapons here and there, she's not going to find anything incriminating. I haven't gotten to where I am today by being stupid and leaving evidence where just anyone can find it.

"I... ah... why do you have so many..." She leaves her words hanging between us.

"It's Vegas. I own three casinos on the strip. Three of the biggest casinos in the state, Charlotte. There are, let's say, less-desirable people that would like to take what I've got," I explain.

Her brows knit together. "Are you in danger?"

"Danger lurks everywhere, sweetheart, especially the desert. But I'm very capable of taking care of myself. Trust me, I'm not going anywhere anytime soon." I smile, trying to ease some of her worry. Which I'm not sure is for me or for herself.

"It would be my luck to find someone like you and then have you disappear," she murmurs before quickly adding, "Shit. Not that I intend to keep you or anything. Or that this is, well, more."

"It could be more," I tell her.

What the fuck am I doing? I should kick her out and erase this fucking fixation I have with her. She's going to be a liability. Everyone in my line of work knows you don't keep anyone around you can't afford to lose. It's why I've never been the relationship type of guy.

"You don't even know me, and as you've seen, I'm a mess." Charlotte turns towards the window, walking over and staring down at the city below us. "Is it always this busy here?"

"Always," I say, standing next to her, my hands in my pockets to stop myself from reaching out to touch her. I need to slow down, for her sake. I'm not usually a patient man. I don't give a fuck what anyone thinks.

I have a feeling that method isn't going to work

with Charlotte, though. And I don't know if this fascination is going to wear off. Or just get worse. It's almost like an illness. The more time I spend with her, the more I want her.

"It's nothing like home," Charlotte says.

"What's home like?" I turn to look at her. I wonder if she's homesick already.

"Suffocating," she says on a long exhale. "Here, I don't feel trapped. There's something freeing about just being part of the crowd, you know."

"I've only ever lived here," I admit.

"Oh, are your parents here too?" she asks me.

"My parents are dead."

"Oh my gosh, I'm so sorry." Charlotte's face drops, sympathy written all over it.

"Don't be. I don't remember them," I lie. I don't remember *my father*. I never knew who he was. But I remember my mother. That's not something I want to talk about right now, though. Or burden Charlotte with.

"I'm sorry. So you don't have any family?"

"I have Sammie and Carlo. They're about as close to family as I need," I explain.

"Well, maybe one day you'll have your own family," Charlotte suggests.

The memory of the empty pill packet left on the counter in her room flickers through my mind. Guess that family won't be starting just yet.

"Maybe," I say at the same time the doorbell rings through the penthouse. "That'll be dinner. Come sit down." I take Charlotte's hand and lead her over to the table before going and opening the door.

"Sir." The waiter nods at me. "Where would you like it?"

"Dining room. Thanks." I pull a hundred out of my pocket.

I treat my staff well. I make sure they're paid decent and I always make an effort to be polite. I find they stay loyal when they're treated well. Don't get me wrong, there's also a healthy amount of fear that I make sure remains firmly in place amongst the staff. They know who I am. They know what I'm capable of.

Once the waiter leaves, I start taking the silver domes off the plates. "Are you expecting more people?" Charlotte questions.

"I have you here. Why the fuck would I need anyone else?" I ask her.

"This is a lot of food, Louie." She laughs.

I pause my movements and look at her, listening

to the sound of her laugh. "I didn't know what you'd like," I tell her when she looks up at me.

"Okay, next time, maybe ask? Because there's no way we're going to be able to eat it all. It seems wasteful," she says.

It is, but when you've come from not having any food, it's always a good thing to have too much. I don't say that, though.

"Okay, next time, I'll ask." I sit down across from her.

"Am I taking you away from your work? I really am okay now. I know I was... Well, before I was... I just wasn't expecting you to come back. If I'd known, I would have tried harder to keep my shit together."

"I don't want you to keep your shit together. If you want to cry, then cry. If you want to scream and smash things, then do that too. If you want to stab someone, make sure you hit a vital organ so they don't get back up." I smirk.

"I'm good," Charlotte says.

"Would you want to see him?" I ask, keeping my tone nonchalant while piling some steamed vegetables onto her plate.

"Who?" Her brows knit in confusion again.

"Your ex? Hypothetically, if he turned up here looking for you, would you want to see him?" My breath pauses, waiting for her answer. I don't know why I care.

If she says yes, I should let her know he's here. I shouldn't stand in her way, right?

Fuck that. I'm not going to let that fucker sweet talk her after what he did. If I have to make sure she doesn't have a chance to see him, I will.

Chapter Fourteen

Charlotte

Do I want to see Owen again? The visual of the gun and all the knives that were in that drawer I opened makes me think yes. I'd love to see him, have him held down, and use one of the knives to cut off his useless dick. Except I'm not that person. I want Owen to crawl into a hole and never appear in my life again.

Reality is, that's not going to happen. But do I want to see him right now?

"Absolutely not," I say with certainty. "I mean, I'd like to see him in the street and mow him down with my car. Maybe reverse over him to make sure he's really dead, you know. But, no, I do not want to see him."

Louie looks at me tentatively for a moment. "If you want him gone, for good, I can make that happen," he says with an eerie seriousness.

I laugh, because I want to believe he's joking. "Don't do that. Plus, he's a cop with cop friends. I doubt they'd take lightly to him going missing."

"Well, say the word and I'll do whatever you want me to do." Louie shrugs.

"He's already here, isn't he?" I ask.

I know Owen. I knew it wouldn't take him long to chase after me. He'd hate the embarrassment of standing in that church waiting for a bride who didn't turn up. I can only imagine the excuses he made, what he said about me to save face.

"He was asking around downstairs. He didn't get any confirmation that you're actually here." Louie says. "He also won't be able to enter this casino again without a warrant, which he won't get."

"Okay, thank you. But he'll get that warrant. I

should probably call him. He won't leave until he tries to talk me into going home and fixing what I did."

"You didn't do anything," Louie growls. *Yes, growls.*

"I left him standing at the altar waiting for me. I told my sister I wanted to make a grand entrance and to ensure nobody came looking for me. I wanted him standing in that church. I wanted him to feel a tenth of the humiliation I felt when I saw them." The tears are burning my eyes. I'm not going to let them break free again, though. Inhaling, I pick up the glass of water in front of me and swallow down the cool liquid.

Louie tilts his head. "Is he... abusive? Are you afraid of what he'll do if you do see him?"

I laugh. "Owen? No, he's never been abusive. He... is set in his ways and has a knack for talking me into doing things I don't necessarily want to do. I've been a pushover. I know that, and I know it makes me sound weak."

"You're not weak. A weak woman would have walked down that aisle, Charlotte. You chose yourself. That's not weak," Louie tells me.

"Why are you so good at this?" I ask him.

"At what?" he questions.

"Talking? Why is it so easy to talk to you?" I don't understand how I'm sitting here spilling my guts to someone I just met, when I can't even bring myself to pick up my phone and call any of my friends.

"You'd have to be the only person on earth who would say I was easy to talk to." Louie laughs.

"Well, I appreciate you listening to me," I tell him. "What would you normally be doing? Like right now, if you weren't sitting here with me?"

"I'd be out walking the floor, talking to high rollers, making sure they were spending as much of their money as possible."

"Sounds fun." I smile, trying to be positive. I honestly couldn't think of anything worse than talking to a bunch of rich people with so much cash they can blow it on gambling.

Louie chuckles. "It makes me money. I wouldn't call it fun."

"Do you think you should be downstairs now? I wouldn't want you to be losing money."

"I'm good. I'd much rather be sitting here with you," Louie says, and then his phone rings. "Shit. I have to take this. Eat. You've barely touched your food." He points at my almost-full plate as he stands up and walks out of the dining room.

I don't think I can eat. My stomach isn't feeling great. My emotions are all over the place and my mind is spinning. I don't know what I'm doing here. I know I need to make some hard decisions. I just don't know if I'm ready to make them yet.

"I'm really sorry. I have to step out for a bit." Louie stops at the table. "Will you be okay? I can get one of the guys to come up and keep you company."

"No, I'm good. I'll go back to my room. I think I just want to lie in bed and binge some crappy television show." I stand and push the chair in. "Wait... Do you want me to do something with all this? I can pack it away."

"Leave it. I'll have someone come and clean up, but you don't need to go. Come with me." Louie takes my hand in his and starts leading me down a hall. Into a bedroom. His bedroom. I can tell because it smells like his citrus aftershave. "You can binge watch whatever you want in here. Make yourself at home," he says, pulling the covers back.

I stare at the bed and then up at him. "You want me to stay here? In your bed?"

"I want to come back and see you right here. So, yes, I want you in my bed," Louie says.

Well, crap. Did my knees just wobble? I think they did.

"Okay," I whisper, climbing onto the plush mattress.

"I'll be back as soon as I can. If you need anything, call me." Louie kisses my forehead and then hands me a phone. My phone.

"Where did you get this?" I ask him.

"Your room. I picked it up before we walked out. My number's on here," he says, handing me a business card.

"Thank you." I dip deeper into what has to be one of the most comfortable beds I've ever been on.

"Here." Louie passes me a remote after he presses a button that makes a screen start descending from the ceiling like magic. "See you soon."

"Um, yeah. Thanks again," I say as he walks out.

I wait until I hear the door click shut. And that feeling of utter aloneness sinks in again. I hate it. Burying myself under the covers, I click on the Netflix app on the television and start scrolling.

After about thirty minutes of not being able to settle on anything to watch, I toss the remote to the other side of the bed in frustration. Then I pick up my phone and turn it on for the first time since I messaged my mom. As soon as the screen lights up, notifications come rapid fire. Ignoring the ones from Owen and my sister again, I open the one from my mom.

> MOM:
>
> Charlotte, call me. Answer your phone, please. We can fix this. We just need to talk about it.
>
> MOM:
>
> Charlotte, you're being really selfish right now. Call me. Let me know that my daughter is alive.

The texts continue. I can tell my mom is worried about me. There's also the sense that she wants to talk me into going home. I don't think I'm going to, though. I'm seriously considering taking Louie up on his offer to stay here and figure out the next chapter in my life.

My finger presses over my mom's name and the dial sound starts ringing out through my speaker.

"Charlotte, is that you?" My mom's voice is rushed.

"It's me, Mom," I whisper.

"Oh, sweet Jesus. Thank god you're okay. You are okay, aren't you? Where are you?" Mom asks.

"I'm okay. I'm just going to stay away for a little bit. I need time," I tell her.

"Time for what? You need to come home and sort out this mess, Charlotte. You know your sister hasn't stopped crying. She's been trying to call you." My mother's concern quickly turns into her reprimanding me.

"You can't be serious right now, Mom. Melanie slept with my fiancé. The night before my wedding. And you're taking her side?" I shout through the phone as anger courses through me.

"I'm not taking anyone's side. I just want you to think about forgiveness. Owen loves you. He's looking for you now. He's a good man, Charlotte."

I can't believe my ears. "I don't want to hear what kind of man you think he is. If he's that good, and you're that desperate to have him in our family, have Melanie marry him because I won't be."

"Charlotte, please. You're upset..." Mom starts.

"No. I'm beyond upset. I'm furious. I'm humiliated and I'm just done, Mom. I'm not coming home yet. I'll reach out when I'm ready." I cut her off and then disconnect the call. I can't believe she had the nerve to tell me I needed to forgive them.

That's not happening anytime soon. If ever.

Scrolling through the other messages on my phone, I click on the group chat I have with my two closest friends. Other than my sister, Rachel and Evie have always been there. I should have called them sooner. Or at the very least, sent them a text.

There's a bunch of missed messages and calls from each of them. I don't know what to say, so instead of saying anything, I send them the video. The same one I sent my mother.

It only takes a minute before my phone lights up with a video chat request from Rachel.

"What the actual fuck? I'm going to kill them. Both of them. It will be slow. I knew something bad had happened. Wait! Where are you?" She finally stops, and I smile.

Yep, I definitely should have put my pride aside and called my friends sooner.

"Are you okay? Tell me that's some sick AI video and it's not real." Evie's face pops up on the screen next.

"I'm okay. Humiliated," I tell them. "And it's not AI. Unfortunately. I filmed it myself."

"Oh my god. Charlotte, I'm so sorry. What a shit excuse for a human. Evie, get the shovels ready. We have some holes to dig," Rachel says.

"Don't do that. I just want to forget. I want to... I don't know what I want. But I want to forget that image," I whisper.

"Oh, honey, I'm sorry," Evie says. "Where are you? We can come to you. Girls' slumber party?"

"I'm in Vegas," I tell them.

"What are you doing in Vegas?"

"Charlotte, I got something for you." Louie walks back into the room, holding up a swimsuit. I wasn't expecting him back so soon.

"Who is that?" Rachel whispers.

Louie comes over to the bed and pops his head around. "Friends?" he asks me while eyeing my screen.

"Uh-huh." I nod.

"Sorry. I didn't know you were on the phone. I'll leave this here. When you're ready, I'll be in my office." Louie leans in and kisses my forehead, and I think I melt a little. Then he just walks away, leaving me in his room with the swimsuit on the bed.

"Who is that? Charlotte? What's happening?" Evie asks.

"Who indeed? And does he have a brother?" Rachel adds.

"Ah, that was... Louie. A friend. He's letting me stay with him for a few days."

"Since when do you have a friend named Louie? A hot friend named Louie who kisses your forehead like you're in some kind of Hallmark Christmas movie?"

"Since I met him here in Vegas. I gotta go. I just wanted to let y'all know I was still alive. I'll call you back later."

"We're coming to find you," Rachel says before I disconnect the call and power down my phone again.

Chapter Fifteen

Louie

I was furious that I had to leave Charlotte alone when she was so clearly upset. I didn't have much choice, though. I can't allow myself to appear distracted or preoccupied. The moment I do, that's when the vultures will come swooping in.

I made quick work of setting an example with the asshole caught counting cards at the blackjack table. Nobody cheats in my casino and leaves unscathed.

I didn't kill him, as much as I wanted to. I let him walk out. Bloody and bruised and with a limp that said what I didn't have to. He won't dare step foot in one of my establishments again. He also will send a message to anyone else looking to cheat me.

It's true what they say about casinos. The house always wins. Sure, some patrons rake in a little cash. It's gambling. It's what keeps 'em coming back for more. In the end, we all know who the real winner is, though. It's how it's always been, how it always will be. After all, Vegas wasn't built on losing money.

The little shit felt the brunt of my frustration tonight. Carlo had to pull me back at one point so I didn't kill the kid. After that, I left, telling him to deal with it.

It was on my way back up that I had the idea of making a quick detour. The one thing I know that will make Charlotte feel better is swimming. When she's in the pool, she seems so carefree. But fuck if I'm going to let her go without a bathing suit again. Which is how I found myself in a boutique asking the staff for a swimsuit. I vetoed the two-piece options they tried to show me and settled for a black one-piece.

I'm currently sitting in my office, pretending to work while I wait for her to come out of the bedroom. I left her to chat with her friends. I'm guessing she hasn't spoken to them since she ran. As long as they're not talking her into returning home, she can keep chatting with them.

Now that I've decided I want to keep her, there are no lengths I'll stop at to make it happen.

The soft tap at my door has me looking up at the one person I actually want to see. "Fuck me. That suit was supposed to cover your body, not make me want to bend you over my desk and rip it off you," I grunt. So much for the one-piece being less attractive to look at. It does nothing to hide her curves.

"Um, okay." Charlotte shrugs and walks towards me. I push my chair back, giving her space as she jumps up and sits on top of my desk. Right in front of me. "This desk right here?" She taps a hand on the spot next to her.

"Uh-huh." My hands part her legs as I stand and fill the space between them. "This desk right here," I repeat.

"Mmm, as tempting as that sounds, I kinda really want to swim," she says, her palms landing on my chest. "Although we could swim after, right?"

"We could. But it's late, and once I get you

naked, I'd want to keep you that way for hours. Let's go up to the pool, and then continue this..." My lips trail along her bare shoulder. "After."

Fuck me. I groan as I tear myself away from her.

"Just so you know, I usually have a lot more self-restraint," I tell Charlotte as I pick up her hand and tug her down from the desk.

"You just turned me down. I'd say your restraint is just fine," she counters.

"Sweetheart, that was not me turning you down. That was me choosing your happiness over my own," I clarify. "Make no mistake, I want you more than I've ever wanted anyone."

"Oh..," she says, and I see the shock on her face. I've done it again. Come on too fucking strong. "Wait... What do you mean you're choosing my happiness?"

"The few times I've seen you swimming, you look happy, content, at peace. I want that for you," I explain while leading Charlotte towards the door. Stopping at the rack, I pick up my coat and cover her body with it. "As great as you look in that swimsuit, I don't need anyone else seeing it."

"Okay," she says. "I do like the pool. I don't know what it is about being in the water, but it's calming."

Charlotte follows me into the elevator. "Thank you for doing this for me."

Sitting on the sun lounger, I watch Charlotte glide through the water. When her head pops up at the other end of the pool, she smiles. A real fucking smile. "You sure you don't want to come in?" she asks me.

"I'm enjoying the view from here," I tell her. If I get in that water, I'll have her pressed up against the edge before driving my cock into her.

"Your loss." She shrugs, pushes off the wall, and flips onto her back.

Yes, it is my fucking loss.

"Hey, boss..." Carlo and Sammie walk up, taking a seat on each side of me.

"How'd you know where I was?" I ask them. "And keep your fucking eyes off her." I growl when I notice the way their eyes drift over to the pool, where Charlotte is floating on her back.

"Were you hiding from us?" Carlo asks.

I shake my head.

"I figured if you weren't in the penthouse, you'd be up here," Sammie says, and I lift a curious brow.

"There a reason for this visit?"

"Can't some friends just pop in and hang out?" Carlo questions while holding up a bottle of whiskey.

"What he said," Sammie adds, moving a tray towards Carlo. A tray with *four* glasses.

"You expecting someone?" I question him.

"Nope, but I figured you'd have your girl here. Wouldn't be the great friends we are if we left her out, now would we?" Carlo chuckles.

I'm about to answer, but then Charlotte decides to pull herself up out of the pool. I jump from my seat and grab a towel while glaring at my two friends, who are getting far too much entertainment out of my annoyance at them.

"I... um, I can go," Charlotte says in a quiet voice.

"You're not going anywhere. If anyone is leaving, it's those two fuckwits, not you," I tell her as I wrap the towel around her shoulders.

"Are you sure? I don't want to be in the way," she whispers.

"You're not. Come on. The sooner I let them talk to you, the sooner they'll be out of our hair." I guide Charlotte over to the lounger. Sitting and pulling her down with me as I settle her between my legs. My arm wraps around her waist, my face buries into her neck, and my tongue darts out to lick a few water droplets.

Charlotte squirms in my hold.

"So, Charlotte, how'd you two meet?" Carlo gestures a hand from me to my girl.

"Ah, I was downstairs at one of the bars feeling sorry for myself, and he sat at my table," she says. "How'd y'all meet each other?"

"We grew up on the streets together," Sammie replies.

"On the streets?" Charlotte parrots.

"He means we've known each other since we were kids," I correct while shooting a glare in Sammie's direction.

"Okay, well, I for one am glad you turned up. I was starting to worry that our boy here was destined to be a bachelor forever and die a lonely old man." Carlo pours whiskey into four glasses, handing one to Charlotte first.

"You don't have to drink that," I tell her.

Looking over a shoulder at me, Charlotte downs the contents of her glass in one go. "I'm from the south. We know how to drink whiskey." She smiles at me.

"Okay then." I chuckle, taking my own glass from Carlo.

"What do you do, Charlotte? For work?" Sammie asks.

"I'm a personal assistant, or I was," she says.

"Did you like your job?" Carlo chimes in.

"I was good at it. I liked helping people." She shrugs.

"Well, it just so happens I have an opening for an assistant if you're looking for work while you're here," Sammie tells Charlotte.

"She's not working for you, asshole. I've already hired her," I cut in.

"You've never had an assistant," Carlo states.

"I've never met anyone smart enough for the role," I reply. "She's not working for either of you two fuckers."

"I... ah..."

"Just go along with it," I whisper into her ear.

"Yeah, sorry, I already accepted a position with Louie," she says without missing a beat.

"Yeah, what are you going to be doing?" Sammie asks her.

"Helping him take people's money, making sure people are... you know... gambling and whatever as much as possible. What else does one do in a casino?" Charlotte throws the question back at him.

"Okay, well, this has been great and all, but it's late and we've got plans that do not involve you two." I stand, my arm firmly wrapped around Charlotte's waist so she's standing with me. "Catch up with you later."

I wave to my friends and take Charlotte's hand in mine. The quicker we get away from these fuckers and their questioning, the better. I trust them as much as I trust anyone, but I don't want to risk anything being said that could lead this woman to find out who I really am.

Chapter Sixteen

Louie takes me up to his penthouse and straight back into his office. "Do you have work to do? I can leave you alone," I tell him. Although, judging by the way his hand tightens around mine, I don't think he wants me to leave.

"Are you tired?" he asks.

I shake my head.

"Good, because I promised you we'd continue where we left off before. I'm a man of my word, Charlotte." He reaches behind my neck and tugs on the straps of my swimsuit. He then slides the wet fabric down my body until I'm standing in front of him completely naked. And one hundred percent onboard with whatever he's cooking up in that sexy head of his. "Fuck me, you're fuckably gorgeous," he growls. There is no other way to describe the noise he makes. Louie spins me around so my front is facing the desk. "I'm going to take my time exploring every single inch of you," he says into my ear as his lips trail up my neck.

"Mmm... that sounds like a good plan."

"Best plan I've ever had." His hand lands on my upper back and pushes down until my front is pressed against the top of his desk.

"Ah... you might want to move all these papers," I suggest. I have no idea what they are—reports of some kind from what I can see.

"Fuck the papers. They can be reprinted." The heat of Louie's body leaves my back and then I feel his grip on my thighs, spreading my legs wider apart.

A moan slips out of my mouth when he drags his fingers through my wet folds, right from my clit to my ass, before he circles my puckered hole.

What the hell is he doing? I start to lift my head when Louie presses one palm on my back, keeping me in place.

"You ever been fucked here before?" he asks, his finger still exploring that forbidden hole.

"N... no..." My voice shakes. Surely, he isn't going to...

"Good. I'll be the first," he says, his tone lifted by a hint of... *joy?*

"Ah, Louie, I don't think..." My words trail off when his tongue slides up the length of my pussy. From top to bottom.

"Trust me, Charlotte, you're going to love every filthy, forbidden thing I do to this body of yours. I guarantee it," he says.

"Oh shit! Oh god!" I moan when his tongue starts lapping at my back hole. This isn't right. But damn, it's good.

Am I this kind of girl?

Three days ago, I would have said absolutely not. Now? I think Louie might be right. I'm going to love everything he does, and I'm going to let him use my body in ways it's never been used before.

His finger pushes in, replacing his tongue. And I freeze, until his mouth moves to my clit. "Oh my god, I think you're trying to kill me." I cry out as a tsunami of pleasure crashes right through my every nerve ending.

"Not kill you. But devour you, yes." Louie stands, my body left limp over the desk before he picks me up from around the waist and flips me over so I'm now lying on my back, looking up at his smiling face. "I'm going to own every fucking part of you, Charlotte. There won't be an inch of your skin or soul I won't consume."

"I think I might let you," I whisper. I'm pretty sure it's not a wise thing to do. Let someone own me the way this man wants to. And the moment his cock lines up with my entrance, I freeze again. "Condom," I remind him. I'm not making another trip to the clinic.

"Right, sorry," Louie grumbles and fusses around in the drawer next to him, until he finds what he's looking for. Much to my relief. At first.

Why does he have those in here? Oh god, does he bring other women in here? Of course he does. A man like Louie isn't the settling down type. I'm more than likely one of a million vaginas that have sat on this desk. My nose scrunches up in disgust.

"What are you thinking right now?" Louie asks as he sheaths his cock.

"How many vaginas have sat on this desk before me?" I blurt out.

Louie's eyebrows rise. "None." He chuckles. "I don't make a habit of bringing people into my home."

"If you don't bring them here, where do you take them?" I question, curiosity getting the better of me. I really don't think I want to know. But I also do at the same time.

"I own three hotels on the strip, Charlotte," Louie says in way of explanation.

"So, you just take women to hotel rooms? Why am *I* here then?"

"You're different," he tells me while lining himself up again. Only to pause and look at me.

"How?" I ask him. "How am I different?"

"I haven't figured that part out yet. I just know that you are." He slowly slides into me until he bottoms out. "Fuck," he hisses. "You good?"

I wrap my legs around his waist, clearing my mind of all thoughts of anyone who *quite literally* came before me. "I'm good."

Louie pulls out and shoves back inside me. "Good. You might want to hold on to something. This is about to get rough," he warns, slamming into me again. Harder than before.

My body aches, but I'm not surprised. I expected it after the night Louie gave me. I woke up alone again. I can't tell if I'm annoyed or relieved. I'd be lying if I said I wasn't a little disappointed. I like his company. I like talking to him. I also know he has his own life and isn't my full-time therapist. Which is why I'm currently tiptoeing towards the front door of his penthouse. I'm not sneaking out. More like... *being considerate*. I don't want to bother him if he's still here.

"Going somewhere?" The deep voice laced with humor has me jumping out of my skin.

Spinning around with a hand on my chest, I gape at Sammie, who is standing just a few feet away from me. "Where the hell did you even come from? And don't do that," I tell him.

"Do what?" he asks.

"Just, poof, appear out of thin air." I snap my fingers to emphasize my point.

"Okay, first, I didn't just appear. I've been here for an hour. Second... well, I don't have a second," he says, shaking his head. "Actually, I do. Where are you sneaking off to?"

"Where's Louie?" I ask, instead of answering him.

"Had an errand to run," Sammie tells me.

"And you're here to babysit me?" I guess.

"Not babysit. Nope, I'm here to keep you company until he comes back."

"Babysit. No thanks. Tell Louie he can call me when he's back. Or not. It doesn't really matter." I shrug, making my way to the door.

"Don't take this the wrong way, but what exactly are your intentions with him?" Sammie asks while following me out of the penthouse.

"My intentions?" I stop at the next suite and swipe my entrance card.

"Yeah, what are your plans with him? Because I gotta be honest, I've never seen him like this and if you're not as into it as he is, then..." Sammie's words trail off. But he's still right behind me when I step into the room I've been staying in—kind of.

"Why are you following me? And what do you mean you haven't seen him like this? What is *this*?" I wave my hands around.

"This is him liking you more than I've ever seen him like anyone. Don't break his heart, Charlotte, because I don't think the city will survive that," Sammie tells me.

"I'm not looking to break anyone's heart. He's known me for days, not years. It's not that serious." I lift a questioning brow. "Are you following me into the shower too?"

"Nope, I like my heart in my chest," he says before making his way over to the sofa. "I'll wait here."

"Suit yourself." I shake my head and walk into the bedroom. I don't think there's much point in trying to get rid of him. I tried that last time and he was relentless.

After spending an hour in the shower—yes, an hour —I decided I needed to go shopping if I'm going to stay in Vegas a bit longer. I need clothes and supplies.

Shit, I'm actually staying.

I pull my phone out of my pocket and send a message to the girls, ignoring the missed calls and texts from everyone else.

ME:

I'm going to stay in Vegas for a bit.
Am I crazy? I'm crazy, right?

RACHEL:

Not crazy. You deserve to choose
you for once.

EVIE:

What she said. Also, I'm booking a
flight. You're not having all the fun
without us.

ME:

I'm okay. Honestly, you don't need
to come here.

I turn my phone back off. It's the only way I can cope with all the messages and calls. By ignoring them.

I'm not surprised to find Sammie still in the living room when I walk out. "I need to go shopping. You want to come?" I ask him. If I pretend that he's just here to hang out and be a new friend—and not my *babysitter*—I can handle his presence a whole lot better.

"Sure. What are we shopping for?"

"Clothes," I tell him. "I came here with nothing. And if I'm staying, I need more than, well, what I have." I have a little bit of savings in my account. I was planning on using it for baby stuff when Owen and I did start a family. I shudder, thinking about the bullet I literally dodged.

The thought of being married to Owen, of having his kids, being stuck... Yeah, I know I was making the right decision when I went to his room that night. Doesn't mean what he and my sister did hurts any less, though.

Chapter Seventeen

Louie

I've never *not* loved what I do. I thrive on the deals made in the shadows, the danger, the power. Not once have I shied away from it or wanted anything different. This is what I've spent my entire life working towards. I don't need to keep going. I have enough money to retire now and never work again. But what the fuck would I do then?

Standing on a dirt airfield about a three hours' drive away from the city, I'm waiting for the plane to land. I'm here to pick up Emmanuel Lopez. The current leader of the De La Sangre Cartel and my contact for the billions of dollars' worth of cocaine I distribute throughout my city.

"You look like you'd rather be doing anything else right now," Carlo says. "You need to keep your head in the game, boss."

"My head is in the fucking game," I grunt at him.

"Jeez, don't shoot the messenger." He holds up his hands. "What's going on with you? You seem distracted lately. And you know what happens when the boss is distracted?"

"I'm not distracted." I'm lying. I am distracted. I know it, and he knows it. But, fuck, if you had an angel fall into your hands *and bed,* you'd be distracted too.

"They get killed. That's what happens, but you know that."

"I'm not getting myself killed, Carlo."

"Not on purpose, you're not. But you will if you don't get your head straight. You know what else happens? When the boss gets killed, what do you think they do to his loved ones?"

"I don't have any loved ones."

162

"Ouch, I'll try not to take that personally. Fine, what do you think happens to his girlfriend?" he asks. "I'll tell you what. They either end up dead with him, after being assaulted and used in ways you don't want to imagine, or they move on with another guy."

I turn and glare at him through the lenses of my sunglasses. Is he looking to get his ass shot right now? "No one other than you and Sammi even knows she exists," I remind him. If I end up dead, I know Sammie will look out for her.

Fuck, I shouldn't even be thinking like this.

First, I'm not getting killed. Second, it's not that serious. "It's also not that serious," I repeat aloud.

"It's not? Could have fooled me." Carlo shrugs. "So I guess you won't care that she's currently at Victoria's Secret with Sammie buying undergarments?" Carlo asks, holding up his phone.

I see the text message from Sammie complaining about being dragged around various shops.

Plucking the phone out of Carlo's hands, I hit dial. "Kill me now," Sammie answers.

"Gladly," I tell him. "Where is she?"

"Well, hello to you too, boss. She's in the dressing room," he says.

"Why the fuck are you in a fucking lingerie store

163

with my girlfriend? My naked girlfriend. Fuck it! I *am* killing you!" I yell.

"She dragged me in here. You told me not to leave her side. Also, I'm not in the dressing room with her. I'm not a fucking idiot," he says.

"Put her on."

"Ah, boss?" Sammie questions.

"What?"

"That would mean I'd have to walk into the dressing room," he says cautiously.

"Slide the phone under the door and walk the fuck away," I instruct him, frustration running through me like a wildfire.

It takes a minute. But then I hear her sweet voice, and I feel almost calm. "Hello? Louie?"

"Charlotte, sweetheart, what are you doing?" I ask her.

"Shopping. What are *you* doing?"

"Picking up a business partner. Why are you in a lingerie store with a man who isn't me?"

"Because I decided I'd take you up on that offer to stay for a bit and I need clothes. Also, I'm a grown-ass woman. And last I checked, you weren't my daddy. I don't need to ask your permission to do anything." She goes on a rant.

"Charlotte, I don't want other men seeing you in various stages of undress," I tell her.

"Again, I have a father, and it's not you. Nice chat. Talk later." The line cuts off.

Did she just...? I check the screen. *She did.*

"She hung up on you, didn't she?" Carlo laughs.

"Fuck off." I hit redial and the phone rings out. So I hit the button again and wait.

"Boss? What'd you say?" Sammie asks.

"Where is she?"

"Changing. She mentioned something about showing you *who's boss?* I don't like this. You know she's scary, right?" Sammie whispers.

"She's a tiny woman."

"With a temper," he adds.

"Get her back to the penthouse. I don't want her anywhere near the casino floor when I walk through with Emmanuel."

"Got it. Keep her off the floor. Should be easy enough," Sammie says—although I hear the sarcasm in his voice.

The sound of a plane hitting the tarmac has me looking up. *Fucking finally.* "Gotta go." I cut the call and hand the phone back to Carlo. "Not a single mention of Charlotte," I tell him as we watch the plane come to a stop at the end of the runway.

"I wasn't born yesterday," he replies.

The hatch door opens and the stairs lower. Ten of Emmanuel's guards step out first, forming a line with a gap in the center. Then their boss follows. "Louie, it's been far too long, my friend," he says, a smile on his face as he steps towards me with outstretched arms.

"It has. How was the flight?" I ask, returning the gesture.

"Bumpy. Thought I was a goner for a bit there." He laughs.

"Let's get out of here. It's fucking hot." I direct him to the cars I have waiting. For both of us.

"Carlo, you're looking old." Emmanuel hugs him.

"Working will do that to you. You should try it sometime," Carlo retorts, and Emmanuel laughs.

"I'll keep that in mind."

"This city never changes." Emmanuel looks up towards the sky.

"From your lips to God's ears," I say. I don't need this city to change. I like it fine just the way it is.

166

"Where's Sammie? He didn't want to come greet me?" Emmanuel asks. I was waiting for it.

Emmanuel, Sammie, Carlo, and I all know each other from our fucked-up childhoods. Emmanuel was the first to climb the ladder. Turns out, his American mother had gotten knocked up by some Mexican drug lord who later tracked him down. Then our friend was shipped off to Mexico and has been coming back and forth to Vegas ever since. Knowing someone that long might give you a false sense of familiarity. Security. Not me, though. I know Emmanuel and I know the cruel bastard he is. His cartel deals in shit I won't touch. But the drugs? They're solid. I won't go anywhere else for them.

"He's working," I reply.

"Right. Well, we'll party tonight. Where we going?"

"Aces." The casino Carlo manages for me.

Emmanuel glances in my direction. I know what he's thinking. Why am I not hosting him here? "What's wrong with the Royal?" he asks. "Am I not worthy of being royal?"

Truth is, I didn't want these assholes anywhere near Charlotte. I'd much prefer to keep her far off Emmanuel's radar. I like the guy. I'll do business with him and entertain him when he's in town. But I won't be able to sit back and watch him do or say anything inappropriate to my girl. And he has a habit of treating women like pieces of meat. A trait he picked up from his old man.

"The new strippers are at Aces," I tell him. "It's also where the game is set for tonight, if you want to buy in." The game being poker. And not just any poker game. All the highest of high rollers want in on this one. I've seen men lose billion-dollar fortunes before. "I've had your bags delivered to Aces."

"I'm staying there too?"

"Yep," I confirm. "Now, come on. Let's get a drink."

I drop a hand on Emmanuel's shoulder as I lead him into the Royal Flush. Not because I want to. But because I know if he thinks I'm trying to keep him out, he's going to want *in* more. And then he's going to dig.

"Carlo, let Sammie know we're here and have him meet us in my office," I call out.

We step inside and Emmanuel takes a seat across

from me. His eyes scanning the room before settling back on mine. "Let's cut to the chase so we can get to the party part of the night. This is Vegas after all," he says, leaning forward. "What do you want, Louie? Why'd you summon me here?"

He's right. I did call him here.

I pour us each a glass of whiskey, sliding one across the desk to him. "I need more product." I look him dead in the eye. His face is a mask of indifference. "The shipments are moving faster than I anticipated. The demand is through the roof."

Emmanuel smirks, taking a slow sip of his drink. "More cocaine, huh? I figured as much. How much *more* we talking?" he asks.

"Double the last order," I reply, watching his reaction.

He leans back in his chair, swirling the whiskey in his glass thoughtfully. "You know the risks involved, Louie. Doubling the shipment means doubling the heat. You really think you can move double?"

I nod, my expression resolute. "I've got everything under control. My network here is solid, and I've taken extra precautions. This is a calculated decision."

Emmanuel's eyes narrow as he considers my request. "All right. I'll make the arrangements. But know this: If anything goes south, it's your head."

"Understood," I assure him. "You'll get your payment upfront, just like always."

He raises his whiskey, a glint of approval in his eyes. "I know I will."

We clink glasses, sealing the deal.

As we finish our drinks, I can't help but feel a mix of anticipation and unease. The stakes are high, but the rewards are even higher. I have my eye on a fourth casino, and I need more cash to get it. This is my way of getting *it* quicker.

"Let's get back to the party," Emmanuel says as he stands. "We've got a lot to celebrate tonight."

We walk outside the office, where Carlo and Sammie are waiting alongside Emmanuel's men. "I'll meet you guys over at Aces. I've got a few things to tie up here," I tell them.

Emmanuel gives me that questioning look again, but he doesn't say anything. Instead, he slaps Sammie on the shoulder and they start chatting like long-lost friends.

I breathe a sigh of relief. *I get it. Why am I doing business with these assholes if I don't want them anywhere near the woman I'm fond of?* Because they've got the best product on the market, and as vile as their cartel can be, others are much worse.

Chapter Eighteen

T he sound of the door opening has me pausing mid-swipe of the hairbrush. Sammie only left a few minutes ago. There's no way he's back already. Before he left, he said: *Under no circumstances are you to leave this room*. I gave him my sweetest smile when I replied with: *Bless your heart*.

I have a feeling he knew exactly what I meant too.

I walk out of the bathroom and pause, watching as Louie enters the bedroom. His eyes rake up and down my body. I'm wearing a shimmery black dress that hugs every single one of my curves. I picked it up today and I love it. Judging by the bulge forming in his pants—one he's doing nothing to hide—Louie likes it too.

Although the fire in his eyes when he finally looks up at me isn't just lust. There's something else there. I just can't put a pin in it.

"Charlotte." He stalks towards me. "You look fucking gorgeous. But don't you think you're a little overdressed for lounging in bed all night?"

"Oh, I have no plans of lounging in bed all night. I want to go out. I want to see what this city has to offer me." I smile at him.

"All this city has to offer is corruption, drugs, human trafficking, and a one-way ticket to hell. You don't need any of that," he tells me.

"That's not true. It has you and you're not bad." I shrug.

A look of uncertainty passes over his face. It's gone within seconds, but I'm sure it was there. "I'm a lot of things. But you are more. And I can't go out with you tonight. I have a meeting with an important client. Which means I really need you to stay put. Better yet, stay put at my place."

"Louie, I need to go out. I've been held back my entire life. I'm finally free. I need to feel alive, to dance, to be around people that have no idea who I am. Who aren't judging me for the whole runaway-bride thing," I try to explain.

Louie steps closer, his expression softening as he reaches for my hand. "I understand that, but it's dangerous out there, especially for a beautiful woman alone. I just want to keep you safe."

He sounds sincere, like he really is worried about me. That's... odd. But also sweet. I still want to go out, though. I appreciate his concern. I just think he's overreacting.

"What if I go and get this meeting done, and when I get back, I'll take you out? We'll dance. We'll get lost in the crowd. Whatever you want," he offers.

I look up at him. "Okay, but you promise you'll come back and go out with me?"

"Promise. Just wait for me. At my place, though. Come on."

I let Louie take my hand as he guides me out of the room and next door to his apartment. "Can I get room service to bring wine up?" I ask him. "Also, just so we're clear on something, this is a onetime thing. I'm not going to just give up my freedom because you have some kind of hangup about me going out alone."

"You can have room service bring up whatever you want," he says, leaning in and kissing my forehead before he adds, "Thank you. I promise I'll be back as soon as I can. Keep the dress on. I can't wait to tear it off you later."

My thighs shake. I don't know if my body can handle another night of Louie's attention. I'm sore. *Everywhere.* But the thought of what I know he can do...? Yeah, *that* has me forgetting all about the pain I'm currently in. It also has me wanting to drag the man into the bedroom right now. His meeting can wait a few minutes or hours, right?

"Fuck me, you make it hard to walk away," Louie groans. He presses his lips against mine. "I'll be back. Stay inside the room."

"Have a good meeting," I tell him

Have a good meeting? Really, Charlotte, that's the best you could come up with? God, I'm so stupid.

An hour and three glasses of wine later, I'm sitting in Louie's living room, bored out of my mind. I decide to call the girls. I need to talk to someone.

"You're alive." Evie is the first to answer my video call.

"I am."

"You're dressed up. You going out?" she asks.

"Soon. Hopefully. What's going on back home? How bad is the town gossip about me?" I wince, not sure if I want to know.

"It's not that bad. Where you going?" Evie's change of topic and non-answer tell me the gossip is bad.

"Out dancing. I'm waiting for Louie to finish his meeting."

"Why?"

"Ah, because he wanted to take me out but had a meeting," I tell her.

"Okay, who has meetings this late at night? What does this Louie guy do?" Evie presses.

"He owns a few businesses here," I explain,

while leaving out the part that he owns three whole casinos. I'm not entirely sure, but I don't want them to judge him before they meet him. Even if they aren't likely to meet him.

This fling will live out its time, and I'll go back home. It's not that serious.

"Why do you look like you have the weight of the world on your shoulders?" Rachel asks, her face appearing on the screen.

"She's going out with Louie when he finishes his nighttime meeting. Oh, and we learned that Louie owns businesses in Vegas. But Charlotte is being sketchy about the details of what those businesses actually are," Evie fills Rachel in.

"I'm not being sketchy. It's just not that serious. I don't care what he does anyway. He's nice to me. Like really nice. I don't think I remember ever being treated the way he treats me, and he barely knows me," I admit.

"So, he's good at sex then," Rachel says.

"The best I've had." I laugh. "It's next level, like things I've never ever thought of doing before."

"What sort of things?" Evie questions.

"Yeah, I'm not talking about that." I can feel my face heating up. "So, what are y'all up to? I miss you."

"I was getting ready to jump into bed. I've got an early start tomorrow," Rachel says around a yawn. She's a pediatric surgeon in her first year of residency. She works really long hours.

"What about you? Where are you going?"

"I don't know. Just out. Dancing," I tell her.

"Why aren't you out exploring the town while you wait for this Louie guy?" Rachel asks.

"He didn't want me going out alone." I shrug.

"And you agreed? Charlotte, you just got out of a long-term relationship with someone who was suffocating you. Do not let someone else do the same thing," Evie says.

"You're right. I'm not going to. I don't know the guy. Why am I doing what he wants? Just because he can give mind-blowing orgasms? Well, guess what? So can my vibrator," I rant.

"You go, girl!" Rachel whoops.

"I'm going out," I tell my friends as I grab my things and walk out the door. "I'll call you both later. Love you."

"Love you. Go get 'em." Evie laughs before I disconnect the call.

I don't know why I so easily fall into the habit of doing what other people want me to do. I need to remember that I'm an adult. I can do whatever I want. I don't need to answer to anyone.

This is the internal pep talk I give myself as I walk through the casino before stepping out into the muggy night air. I look up at the sky. You can't see stars here. I miss looking at the stars. Just as I take another step forward, someone grabs on to my arm, yanking me back.

"Where the fuck have you been?" a familiar voice hisses in my ear.

"Ouch, Owen, you're hurting me." I try to free my arm but his grip only tightens as he pulls me away from the entrance towards a darker spot on the street. There are people all around us, but no one is looking our way.

"*Hurting you?* How the hell do you think I felt standing in a fucking church waiting for you? What the hell, Charlotte?" he seethes.

"Yeah? And how do you think I felt walking in to find you fucking my sister?" I push at his chest, and shock has him loosening his grip on me.

"I don't know what you're talking about," he says.

"Really? So *this*..." I pull out my phone and open the video. "...isn't you and Melanie?" I shove the screen into his face.

"Charlotte, baby, this is a misunderstanding. It didn't mean anything. I love you. We can fix this."

"You don't love me. You never did." I shove one more time, and he finally lets go of my arm entirely. "Lose my number and go home, Owen. I don't ever want to see you again," I tell him before running back inside the hotel.

Tears slide over my cheeks as I make my way towards the elevators. I don't know why I'm crying. I'm annoyed that I've let him reduce me to tears again. My hands angrily swipe at my face.

When I get back to Louie's penthouse, I realize I don't actually have a way to get in. So I go to my room and swipe my entrance card. Where I kick off my shoes as soon as I push through the door. The dress comes next. I leave it on the floor in the living room and walk to the bed in nothing but a pair of panties.

So much for my night of freedom, my night of fun. I should have listened to Louie and just waited for him. He's right. This city is full of no-good assholes. My ex being one of them.

Chapter Nineteen

Louie

A week ago, I would have enjoyed the scene in front of me. Beautiful, scantily-clad women everywhere. Now, all I want to do is go home to Charlotte. These chicks are doing nothing for me. Although judging by the smile on Emmanuel's face, he's very happy with the night's entertainment.

He leans forward with a grin. "Who is she?"

"Who is who?" I look around, expecting him to point to one of the girls in particular.

"The one who has your balls in her clutches. You haven't even blinked at any of 'em." He waves a hand around the room. "And I know you. If you're not interested in anything on the menu here, you have someone else. Who is she?"

"*She* is none of your business," I tell him. My jaw clenches.

"Ah, so I was right. You went and found yourself a wife." He laughs. "Never thought I'd see the fucking day."

"I don't have a wife." I roll my eyes.

"If she's special enough for you to want to hide her from your friends, and you clearly aren't interested in other options, then maybe she should be made a wife," he says.

"What the fuck would you know about wife material? Your longest relationship has been... what? Five hours?" I retort.

Emmanuel shrugs. "I don't have a need or a want for a wife."

"And I do?" I raise a brow at him, bringing my glass to my mouth.

"If you found someone willing to put up with

your sorry ass, keep her. She's clearly one of a kind." The asshole laughs again. This time louder.

"Fuck off. It's not that serious," I say, and I'm not sure if the lie is for my own benefit or his.

"Sure it's not. Where is she?" he asks.

"Not here," I grunt at him.

Emmanuel squints his eyes at me. "You don't trust me? I'm hurt," he says with a hand over his heart.

"I don't trust anyone. You know that."

"We've been friends for a long time, Louie," Emmanuel reminds me. "There are very few people I would consider a friend. You are one of them. I wouldn't do anything to someone important to you."

"Unless you wanted to get at me for something," I tell him. "Women and children aren't off-limits in your organization."

"Then I guess you best not give me a reason to hurt you." He smiles at me. "*Relax*. Things are changing in Mexico. My tyrant father is dead."

"Yeah, and how'd that go down, exactly?" I ask him. The old man was killed a few months ago, leaving my friend here in charge.

"Better you don't know. Like I said, I don't want to have to kill you," Emmanuel tells me. "Now, get out of here. You look sad and you're scaring away the girls."

I glance at Sammie and Carlo, who are sitting across from us. "I'm out. You got this?" I ask them. They nod, and I take that as my cue to leave while I can. I return my focus to Emmanuel. "I'll catch up with you tomorrow. Welcome back to town."

It's still early. I promised to take Charlotte out dancing. It's the last thing I want to do. I'd much rather keep her occupied in my bed. But if dancing is what she needs, then dancing is what she'll get.

I know it as soon as I walk through the door of my penthouse. *She's not here.* The place has that eerie quietness. *Where the fuck did she go?*

I walk back out and unlock the door to the room I set her up in. I really need to find a way to get her to just stay at my place.

I find her in the bed. Asleep. Odd, seeing as I really thought she wanted to go out. I lean over, pull the blankets down, and scoop her up. This won't do. I need her in my bed. Why would she come back here? If she was tired, she should have just climbed into my bed.

Charlotte's eyes slowly blink open as I walk down the hall towards my door. "Louie, what's going on?" she asks, her voice groggy.

"I'm taking you to bed. Go back to sleep," I tell her, leaning down as I kiss the middle of her forehead. It's not a gesture I've done before I met her. On her, though, it feels right.

I sound like a fucking pussy. I probably need my head examined. Because this shit, the feelings she's evoking within me... are not normal. They're so foreign I don't know what I'm supposed to do with them. The only thing I know for certain is that I want her with me as much as humanly possible right now.

I'm not suggesting that it won't wear off—although the few times I've had to step away from her leave me wanting more, not less. I've never been a believer in witches or magic or curses, but maybe there's merit to all that hocus-pocus shit. She's either put some kind of spell on me or this is God's way of fucking with me.

I know I'm not a good person, so why the fuck would they put an angel in my path? Why would they put someone as pure as Charlotte here for me to claim as mine? The only reason would be to punish me, and they'll do that by showing me goodness and then ripping it away.

I hold on to her tighter. Fuck anyone who thinks I'll let her go without a fight, God or not.

I lay Charlotte down and pull the blankets up. "Are you coming to bed?" she asks me.

"I'm gonna shower real quick. Go back to sleep," I tell her.

By the time I finish rinsing off and changing into something clean, Charlotte's out of it again. Her light snores fill the room. Making my way over to the bed, I'm about to flick the light off when she rolls over and something catches my eye. Not something. A mark. On her upper arm. I lean closer to see exactly what it is. A fucking handprint. Someone had their hand wrapped around her arm tight enough to leave a fucking bruise.

"Charlotte, wake up." My voice is harsher than I intended it to be, as a red haze takes over my vision.

She jumps and her eyes snap open, bouncing around the room before settling on me. "What's wrong?"

"Who did this to you?" I hiss through gritted teeth while gesturing to her arm.

Charlotte looks down and then back at me. "It's nothing," she says.

"I didn't ask what it was. I asked who did it. Who the fuck put their hands on you?" I'm already moving around the room, putting on the pants and shirt I just took off. I can feel her watching me.

"What are you doing? Why are you mad?"

"Answer the question, Charlotte. I want to know who did that," I tell her as I continue to pace back and forth across the carpet.

"I... I went outside, and Owen was there. He wanted to talk to me," she says.

I pull out my phone and call Sammie. He answers on the second ring. "Boss?"

"Round up Carlo and Emmanuel. We have a hog to roast."

"What? Fuck? Really? You sure?" Sammie asks.

"Do I sound un-fucking-sure?" I yell before hanging up. Then I storm into my closet, pulling the suits aside to unlock the safe. I reach inside and grab a pistol and a knife.

"Wait... Why do you have a gun?" Charlotte is behind me. "Why do you have all those guns? That's a lot of guns, Louie. What are you doing?"

"Go back to bed," I tell her.

"Oh, sure, I'll just go back to bed when my

boyfriend seems to be losing his damn mind and is... What *are* you doing? Loading up with weapons?" she asks me.

I pause and spin around. She's standing in the doorway of my closet, wearing nothing but a pair of black lace panties. "Say it again," I groan.

"What are you doing?" she repeats.

"Not that part. The boyfriend thing, say it again." I stalk towards her.

"It was a slip of the tongue. I didn't mean that." Charlotte averts her eyes. "Sorry."

My fingers press under her chin, tipping her face upwards until her eyes connect with mine. "I like it. Being your boyfriend," I tell her. My voice somehow manages to sound calm, even though I'm fired up on the inside.

"You mean that?" she questions before quickly adding, "It's too soon."

"I don't say shit I don't mean. And since we've established you're now my girlfriend, you have to understand that I'm not about to let some fucker get away with hurting you. No one, and I mean no one, puts their hands on you, Charlotte."

Her eyes widen. "You can't do anything to Owen. He's a cop, Louie. You'll get in trouble."

I laugh. "Sweetheart, I don't give a fuck if he's

the goddamn Pope. He hurt you. He's gonna feel that tenfold."

"Please, just come to bed. You're mad, and I'm sorry. I shouldn't have gone out. I should have just stayed and waited for you like I said I would. I don't want you getting into trouble over me. It's not worth it."

"Charlotte, you are more than worth it. Whoever put it into your head that you're not... is a fucking idiot. You. Are. Worth. It," I emphasize, hoping my words sink into her. "I'll be back. Now, go to sleep."

"Louie, this is insane. I told him to go home. He's not sticking around town. Just let it go."

It's on the tip of my tongue to agree with her, for her benefit. I can't lie to this woman, though. "I won't be long." I grab hold of the back of her head and press my lips against her forehead again. "Please stay here," I say and step around her. Stopping at the bedroom door before I turn and look at her again. "Why didn't you come back here? When you came up?"

"I don't have a key to get in." She lifts a shoulder.

Opening my wallet, I pull out the spare master key. "This will get you into any room in any of my casinos," I tell her as I drop the card on to the bedside table. "I want you here when I get back."

By the time I make it downstairs, Sammie, Carlo, and Emmanuel are waiting for me. "You guys ready for a barbecue?" I smirk.

"Always," Emmanuel answers without even questioning why we're about to go after a cop.

"Is she okay?" Sammie asks, knowing it has to have something to do with Charlotte.

"He grabbed her. Fucker left a mark on her," I tell him through gritted teeth.

Carlo's eyes widen, and then he smiles. "What the fuck? Good thing I have a hankering for pork tonight."

"Let's go." Sammie nods at me.

Chapter Twenty

What on earth is happening right now? He just walked out. Louie just walked out of here with a gun. I don't know what to do. I should warn Owen, right? Tell him to get out of town if he hasn't already.

But Louie isn't going to actually kill him. He

wouldn't actually *kill* someone. He looked really worked up, but I don't think he'd do that.

Shit, what if he does? What if he ends up in jail because of me?

Reality crashes into me. I'm more concerned about what's going to happen to Louie, a man I've just met, than I am about Owen, a man I spent the last few years beside. Something is wrong with me.

Where is my phone?

I look around the room and find my cell plugged into a charger on top of the bedside table. Louie must have grabbed it again. I swipe it up and call Evie. I know she'll still be awake—she suffers from severe insomnia—and I don't want to bother Rachel when she said she was going to bed.

"Charlotte, what's happening?" Evie answers right away.

"I messed up," I tell her.

"Okay, but did you do that with clothes on or did that happen afterwards?" she asks me.

I look down at myself. "Shit! Sorry." I forgot I didn't have a top on. Pointing the phone towards the ceiling, I walk into Louie's closet and grab a shirt from the shelf. Ignoring the safe he left wide open. The safe that's filled to the brim with weapons.

Why does one person need so many weapons?

"It's fine. What happened?" Evie presses.

"I went out. I was going to just go out by myself after I spoke to you and Rachel," I tell her.

"Yep, and then what?" She urges me to keep going.

"The moment I stepped outside the casino, Owen was there. He grabbed me and dragged me to the side," I explain.

"He *what*? Are you okay?" Evie starts pacing around her bedroom.

"I'm fine. I told him to go home. That I knew what he and Melanie did. And then I returned to my room and just went to sleep."

"Okay, so how did you mess up?" Evie asks.

"Louie came home. Saw I was there and brought me back to his place, but then he saw the bruise," I tell her.

"What bruise?"

Turning the screen towards my arm, I lift my sleeve to show her the bruise.

"What the hell, Charlotte? Owen did that?" she yells, and I nod.

"Yeah, when he grabbed me. But I'm fine."

"I'm going to kill him," Evie seethes.

"I think Louie might beat you to it," I whisper.

"Good. I hope he does."

"No, Evie, I'm serious. He lost his mind. As soon as he saw my arm, he kept asking me who did it and I told him and then he got dressed and he..." I stop.

Should I be saying all this over the phone?

"He what?"

"He has guns, Evie. He opened a safe in his closet. He took guns. Told me to go to bed and that he'd be back," I whisper.

"Okay, calm down. It's going to be okay," she says. "Wait... Are we even worried about Owen? I mean, he kinda deserves whatever he gets."

"Evie!" I gasp. "We don't want anyone dead."

"Right. You're right." She nods in agreement before adding, "*But...* if anyone has to die, Owen is a good choice."

"Evie? Why would someone have a safe full of guns?" I ask her.

"Ah... I'm not sure, but I have an idea. What did you say Louie's last name was?"

I didn't. I purposely didn't tell them. I didn't want them to know that he owns casinos. I don't want them to judge him for being some rich asshole. Especially because he's *not* an asshole. Well, not towards me anyway. "Louie Giuliani," I tell her.

I hear Evie typing the name into her keyboard. "Holy shit, I mean, I knew he was hot after that quick peek. But, Sweet Mother Mary, this man is fine, Charlotte." She whistles.

"He really is." I sigh.

"Ah... Charlotte?" Evie pauses.

"What?"

"Have you looked him up, like at all?" she asks me.

"No. Why?" I tell her.

"He owns casinos, as in *multiple*. On the Vegas strip."

"I know," I admit.

"There... ah... there are also some articles that suggest he's involved in the criminal underworld," she whispers.

"What? That's ridiculous. Why would he be involved in the criminal underworld?" I ask.

"Why wouldn't he be?" Evie counters. "He's a casino owner. *In Vegas*. He has a safe full of guns, and he's gone after a cop because the guy hurt you."

"Well, when you put it like that, it doesn't sound good. But... he's not a bad person, Evie."

"You don't know him," she reminds me.

"But I know that he's good. He's... I don't know how I know. I just know that he's not bad," I try to explain.

"I think you should come home. I don't like the

idea of you being out there by yourself," Evie says. "You're in bed with a mobster."

"Actually, I'm in bed alone right now," I say, attempting to lighten the mood as I fall onto Louie's mattress. "And it's the most comfortable bed I've ever slept on."

"Probably 'cause it's paid for in blood money." Evie laughs. "Look, I'm just worried about you. But I'm also excited *for you*. It's been a long time since you've done anything for yourself."

"I know." I sigh.

"And if it's a mobster you want to do, then just... maybe learn how to shoot a gun or something. You might need it."

"Funny," I retort.

"I really am booking a flight. I'm coming to see for myself that you're safe."

"What about the store? You can't just leave," I tell her. Evie owns and runs a small boutique in town.

"It'll be fine. I'm coming," she says. "I'll be there tomorrow... or I mean *today*."

"Don't book a room. You can stay with me."

"With the mobster you're shacking up with?" She laughs.

"No, smart-ass, I have my own room here. It's more like an apartment really. It's huge."

"Are you sure? I can book a room," Evie says.

"No, don't waste the money," I tell her.

"Are you going to be okay? Until I get there?"

"Of course. I don't know what Louie is doing, but I don't feel like he'd hurt me, Evie." I pause. "Is it wrong that my first thought is what will happen to him and not Owen?"

"No. Owen's an ass who doesn't deserve to be anywhere in your thoughts."

"I spent *years* with him, Evie. I should still care."

"You didn't love him. I believe you did, at one point, but we could tell your heart wasn't really in it, especially the closer we got to the wedding."

"Why didn't you say anything?"

"We did. Rachel and I both asked you multiple times if you really wanted to get married and you kept insisting you did," she says.

"You're right. I thought that things would change after the wedding. I just thought it was jitters. And then I knew I couldn't go through with it. I was going to tell him the night before."

"I know. But let's focus on the future. You can literally do anything you want now," Evie says.

"Yeah," I agree with a smile. "I've never felt more free."

"Even if you are shacked up with a mobster." She laughs.

"He is not a mobster," I huff. "I love you, Evie."

"Go to sleep. I'll be there soon," she says. "Love you too." Then the camera cuts off and she's gone.

Is my friend right? Is Louie a mobster? It seems so strange to think that he is. Then again, the question I should be asking myself is: *What do I do if it's true? Leave? Stay?*

Chapter Twenty-One

I watch the footage of Charlotte being grabbed around her arm. And not for the first time. I keep hitting replay and I'm not sure why, seeing as all it does is get me more worked up. "I want to know where the fuck he is. Now!" I yell out.

"I'm on it. Scanning his face through every hotel

page 205

CCTV. Wherever he's staying, we'll know about it soon," Carlo says.

I want this cocksucker's head on a spike. I want his hands boxed up and sent to his mother. I want to burn his remains in a shallow fucking grave out in the desert.

"This is a lot of effort for someone who, in your words, *isn't important*," Emmanuel says from where he's seated in a wingback chair, his posture relaxed as he observes me with a close eye.

"Denial is a common theme in this city," Sammie adds.

"Fuck off. I don't care what any of you say. I want this fucker's head, and if I have to do it myself, I will. I don't need your help," I tell all three of them.

"What? And let you have all the fun?" Carlo shrugs. "Besides, I happen to like her."

"Me too, even if she does scare the fuck out of me," Sammie says.

"I think I need to meet this *Charlotte*." Emmanuel looks directly at me. The fucker wants me to know that he knows her name. I've made it a point not to mention it in front of him. And Sammie and Carlo haven't either.

I shake my head. "Sure, when hell freezes over," I tell him.

"She doesn't know," Sammie says casually.

"Doesn't know what?" Emmanuel's interest is piqued. I don't think that's a good thing.

"That the boss here is... Well, she doesn't know what he does. What any of us do."

"What does she think you do, then?" Emmanuel prods.

"Business," I tell him. "And I plan to keep it that way." At least for a while. I don't want to lie to Charlotte, but I do want to keep her around long enough to make it harder for her to leave.

"It's not an easy secret to keep from the woman who is warming your bed every night," Emmanuel states.

"She knows what she needs to know. I don't need her being implicated in anything." I'm not a fucking idiot. I know I can't hide this part of my life from her forever, but I will for as long as I can. For her benefit, not mine.

"Your life, man. What's the game plan here?" Emmanuel asks me. "You know I'm down for anything. I don't give a fuck who this asshole is. You, though, you need to think with your head, not your rage." He points at me.

"I want his fucking head rolling down the

goddamn strip." My fists clench and unclench as I try to rein in my anger.

"I hear that. I do. However, it's not smart. This cop is connected to your girl. He goes missing after coming looking for her, and the first person they're going to focus on is the ex," Emmanuel says. "You want your girl dragged into a station for questioning?"

I don't say anything. I don't need to. I will not let this come back on Charlotte. I also don't need no fucking dirty cops looking her way. "Fine. We do this clean."

"Got him," Carlo says. "He's staying at the Norge."

"Cheap fuck," I grunt. The Norge is one of those pay-by-the-hour joints. Known for street walkers and junkies. "Get me five grams and a syringe." I can't make him bleed or hurt like I'd prefer, not if I don't want this shit to fall back on Charlotte.

"Got it," Sammie says. "I'll meet you there."

With a curt nod, I stand, pick up my wallet, and swallow the last of my whiskey. "Let's go show this fucker what happens when someone touches something that belongs to me."

"Car's waiting." Carlo pushes up from his seat before buttoning his jacket.

"One less pig around here is a brighter world, if you ask me." Emmanuel chuckles as he stands and follows us out of my office.

As we make our way through the casino floor, I'm stopped by a few guests that I exchange quick, polite conversation with before promising to catch up with them later.

I look to my left the moment I step outside. That's where she was standing. Right in front of my own casino. No one should have touched her, especially in my fucking house. In my fucking town.

Maybe I need to make it public knowledge that Charlotte belongs to me. Of course, no one here knows she's mine, which explains why not a single fucking person stepped in to help her when that asshole cornered her. I'm going to fix that, though. Tomorrow night, I'm taking her out and then every fucker will know just how off-limits she is.

"You know, getting wifed up is the best way to put a target on your back," Emmanuel says from where he's seated beside me in the town car, as Carlo climbs into the front passenger seat. "It's announcing to the world that you have a weakness."

I glare at him. "You planning to exploit that weakness?" We might be friends, in a way, but I will put a bullet in this motherfucker's head without blinking if he threatens Charlotte.

"Fucking hell, man, you really need to relax. I ain't gonna touch your girl." He shakes his head.

By the time we get to the motel, Sammie is already waiting out front. He waves a key in our direction. "Room sixty-nine." He smirks.

I slip my hands into a pair of leather gloves and shake my head. "Grow up," I say before snatching the key from him. "No marks. No bruises." I wait for each of them to nod.

"You know, this is just like old times," Carlo says. "The four of us, lurking around in the dark of the night, primed and ready to teach some asshole a lesson."

"Good times," Sammie tells Carlo.

"We were poor and fighting for survival. Not sure I'd classify that as good times," I mutter under my breath.

"You three were poor. I was loaded," Emmanuel says, pointing to himself. "Son of a cartel leader."

"Remind me... what was it that happened to your father?" I ask Emmanuel.

His face doesn't change. No emotion whatsoever. "He got what he deserved."

"Right." I suspect that he killed the old man himself. He'd be fucking stupid to admit that aloud to anyone, though, and Emmanuel is anything but stupid.

I put the key into the door and push it open before rushing into the room. Owen startles but doesn't get up off the crappy plastic chair he's sitting on. "Room's occupied," he calls out, his words slurred.

There's an almost-empty bottle of vodka on the table in front of him. Perfect. The door behind me shuts, and Carlo and Sammie walk up to Owen. Grabbing him by each arm and dragging him onto the bed. The fucker doesn't even fight. He has no sense of self-preservation.

"I got him." Emmanuel replaces Sammie. "You get the shit."

Sammie walks back over to the table, where he pulls out a rock and a spoon and prepares the syringe before handing it to me.

I refocus my attention on Owen as I kneel on the

bed. He eyes the syringe, and something must finally register in his head. "What are you doing?" he asks.

"Sending you to hell. This is for Charlotte. You shouldn't have put your filthy hands on her," I reply.

"What the fuck? She's my fucking fiancée, asshole!" he hisses, and the fact that he thinks he has some sort of claim on her has me seeing fucking red.

"Yeah, well, she belongs to me now," I tell him as I push the needle into his outstretched arm. He thrashes around, trying to break free but he ain't going anywhere with my guys on him. "See you in hell, motherfucker."

I'm careful to keep the syringe hanging out of his arm as I watch the drugs take effect. Then I nod at Carlo and Emmanuel. I don't need to wait around to watch the finale. No one can survive the amount of blow I pushed into the fucker's system.

"Let's go." I head out the door without looking back.

Chapter Twenty-Two

I don't know how long I've been pacing up and down the living room before I hear the door open. I let Evie's whole "he's a mobster" thing get into my head. To the point I Googled Louie's name and read through numerous news articles that suggest he isn't just a mobster but the leader of the Las Vegas underworld.

It's all speculation. Nothing has ever been proven. Which probably means it's just rumors and conspiracy-theory bullshit, right?

He's not a criminal. I'm not sleeping with a criminal. Although, I do see the irony if he was. I just ran from someone who works to uphold the law, right into the arms of someone who breaks it. Someone who profits on breaking it.

I haven't known the man for long. A couple of days isn't long. I get that. But when I look back to when I first met Owen, I don't remember him being as attentive—or as nice. I do remember wondering why Louie's knuckles were bruised, though. I never mentioned it because it's really none of my business. I assumed he works out, boxes, or something. But what if they're bruised because he uses those fists on someone else?

The saying *sometimes good people do bad things* comes to mind. So what if Louie does some bad things? Does that automatically make him a bad person?

Holy shit, my mind is making up excuses for him before I even know if it's true. Does that make me a bad person?

I turn to face Louie when he walks into the living room. My eyes rake up and down his body, searching for... blood splatters? I don't know what, but I don't see anything.

"Charlotte, you okay?" he asks me.

"Are you a mobster?" I blurt out.

Louie's expression goes from one of shock to casual as can be. An *I don't have a care in the world* smirk on his face within seconds. "Why would you ask that?" He walks towards me.

"Nope. Stop." My hand shoots up between us, and to my surprise, Louie actually pauses. He doesn't say anything. Just stands there. We're locked in a silent, staring contest for what seems like forever. He's not going to answer my question. "Are you?" I ask again.

"Am I what, Charlotte?"

"A mobster," I repeat. "My friend Evie Googled you. She's coming here by the way, but that's not the point. Are you a mobster? It's a simple yes-or-no question, Louie. And where did you go just now? Did you do something to Owen?"

"You want a drink?" Louie offers casually, walking over to the bar cart on the opposite side of the room.

"No, I want answers," I tell him.

"Sometimes we think we want answers, but what we really want is reassurance. I think what you want is reassurance that you're not making a wrong choice by staying here with me." He turns back in my direction, his eyes boring right into mine.

Is he right? Do I just want to know I'm making the right choice by staying here?

When I don't say anything, Louie continues. "You aren't trapped here, Charlotte. You are free to leave whenever you like. I'm not forcing you to do anything you don't want to do. I suspect for the first time in a long time, you're making decisions for yourself."

"So if I left right now, you wouldn't try to stop me? You wouldn't follow me?" My heart starts racing. Am I making this whole three-day relationship more than what it is?

"I didn't say I wouldn't do everything in my power to stop you, to convince you. But I'm not holding you here against your will. No matter what kind of monster I am, I'm not that kind," he tells me.

"So you *are* a mobster?" I ask with a raised brow. He admitted as much, even if he didn't use the exact word.

"One thing I won't ever do is lie to you." Louie starts walking towards me again, a glass of amber liquid in his hand. I don't stop him this time. "I also won't tell you anything that could be used against you," he says. "Am I a mobster? No, I'm not affiliated with any mob family."

Something about the way he says that is strange. "What do you mean you won't tell me anything that can be used against me?"

"I will always do everything to keep you safe, Charlotte. There are aspects of my life that I will keep from you, for your own benefit." Reaching for me, Louie cups my face with his free hand. "I would prefer if you didn't get implicated in anything. Please, don't ask questions I really can't answer."

"So what you're telling me is that you're a criminal but won't admit it for my sake, not yours?" He can't be serious right now.

His left eye twitches. *Oh, I must have hit a nerve. Good.*

I have spent enough time putting up with non-answers. Now that I think about it, I should have pushed Owen more about where he was all those times he came home late. He was probably out fucking my sister while I sat at home waiting for him.

"I'm not doing it again," I say, taking a step back from Louie.

"You're not doing what again?" He takes a step forward, closing the gap between us.

"I can't just go along with whatever you say. I

can't be the girl who sits at home, ignorant to the fact her boyfriend is out sleeping with her sister. I can't just take your word that everything is okay. I can't be stupid again," I explain in one long breath.

"First of all, I'm not sleeping with your sister. Nor will I ever sleep with your sister. Or anyone else, for that matter. If I tell you that we're exclusive, then that's exactly what we are. Second, you're far from stupid and I'm not standing here trying to pull the wool over your eyes."

I look up at him. "What happened with Owen?"

Louie's fingers brush over my arm, over the mark my ex put there. "I made sure he can't ever hurt you again," he says. "I won't ever let anyone hurt you, Charlotte. I take care of what's mine."

"And I'm yours?"

"Like it or not, I found you and I plan on keeping you. And just so we're both clear, we..." Louie points between us. "...are doing this, and we are exclusive. I don't share."

"Don't you think this is all happening a bit too fast?"

"Yes," he says. "But I trust my gut. It's never led me astray before. And right now, my gut is telling me to hold on to whatever it is that's growing between us. To nurture it. Because I have a feeling it's going to be something out of this world, something extraordinary even."

"Do you think Carlo was serious about his job offer?" I quickly change the subject.

Louie appears taken aback. More so than when I asked him if he was a mobster. "What? Why?"

"Well..." I smile. "If I'm going to stay, I'll need a job. I have a bit of savings but it's not going to last long."

"Here." Louie takes his wallet from his back pocket and pulls out a black card.

I look from the card in his outstretched hand, up to his face. "What is that?"

"It's a credit card. Whatever you need, put it on this," he says.

"Yeah, I'm not taking that." I shake my head.

"Yes, you are," he insists.

"No, I'm not." I fold my arms over my chest. "I'm not a charity case."

"No, you're my girlfriend and I'm not going to have my *girlfriend* work for some other guy," he says, putting extra emphasis on the title.

"Yeah, I'm also not a whore. You're not paying for me," I tell him.

"What the fuck? How did we go from you're my

girlfriend to you thinking you're my whore?" Louie shakes his head.

"You're trying to pay me. That suggests you're paying me to be your girlfriend. That's the very definition of a whore."

"No, a whore is someone you pay for sex. I want a lot more than just sex from you, Charlotte. I want everything."

He wants everything? That's a problem, considering I'm not sure I have anything left to give anymore. "What if I don't have anything to give you?" I ask aloud.

Louie smiles at me. "Charlotte, you have already given me more than you'll know." His lips press into mine. Soft, gentle.

Damn him and those lips. This man is like a drug. When he's touching me, it's hard to think straight. I know I'm going to have more questions later.

"Let's go to bed. It's late," Louie whispers against my mouth.

"Okay." I sigh. I can't bring myself to walk away, even though my head is telling me I should.

Chapter Twenty-Three

I'm back there. In that alleyway. Huddled between two dumpsters. It's cold, dark, and my stomach is growling. I don't know how long it's been. She's going to come back soon. She said she'd come back soon. Then there's a noise—no, it's not a noise. It's a whimper.

I look next to me. I'm not alone. "Louie, you said I wouldn't get hurt."

"Charlotte, what are you doing here?" I whisper. "You're not supposed to be here."

"I'm here because you're here. I'm hungry, Louie. When can we leave?" she asks me.

"What?" I look around. We're no longer in the alleyway. And I'm not a child waiting for his mother. We're in a casino, crouched down behind a slot machine. "What's happening?" I ask no one in particular.

"I'm scared, Louie," Charlotte says. "I'm hungry and cold and scared."

I wake with a start. My body jolts up in bed. The usual feeling of hunger hits me. Charlotte lies beside me. Asleep. She has to be hungry too. Right? She was there, in the dream. That hasn't ever happened before. No one has seeped into the nightmare before.

What the fuck does it mean that Charlotte was there?

Climbing out of bed, I contemplate waking her

up. She has to be hungry. I should wake her up and make her eat something. Common sense tells me it was just a dream and not real. That she's fine. She's safe. She's not hungry, cold, or scared.

I walk into the kitchen, open the fridge, and pull out one of the ready-made meals. Peeling the plastic off the top and popping the tray into the microwave. My stomach growls, and my fists clench at my sides. I can't stand being hungry. I should be used to it by now. It's not uncommon for me to wake up from one of those dreams starving.

The microwave pings. I grab the tray and sit it on the counter. Before dropping onto one of the stools and digging into the food. I eat fast. I always do when no one is watching. When no one is here to judge. No one knows that, out of all the situations I've encountered in life, I've never been more scared than I was in that alleyway, waiting for a mother who wasn't ever coming back.

The sound of footsteps behind me has my spine straightening. "Louie, it's four in the morning," Charlotte says, her voice groggy from sleep.

I stop eating—although it's the last thing I want to do—and turn to face her. "I'm sorry. I didn't mean to wake you."

"You didn't. I rolled over and the bed was empty.

That's what woke me up," she says, sitting down next to me.

"You're hungry. Let me get you something to eat." I go to stand, and Charlotte grabs hold of my arm. Her hand is freezing.

"I'm not hungry," she says.

"You're cold, Fuck. Shit." I jump up off the stool, run into the living room, and pull the throw blanket off the sofa. I bring it back and wrap it around Charlotte's shoulders. "I'm so sorry," I tell her. "I'll get you some food."

"Louie, stop. I'm fine. Really, I'm not cold and I'm not hungry," she says.

Ignoring her protests, I set another tray in the microwave, keeping my back to her while I wait for the timer to go off. I'm trying to control my need to wrap her up and hold her close to me. I want to apologize for failing her already, for letting her go hungry and cold. That never should have happened.

What the fuck am I doing?

I startle out of my thoughts when the microwave dings. I take the food out, place it in front of Charlotte, and hand her a fork. "Eat. You should never have to feel hunger," I tell her. "I won't let you go hungry." Then I reclaim my seat and pick up my own fork again. Mindful of how fast I'm eating this time.

"Louie, what's wrong?" Charlotte asks me.

"I shouldn't have let you go cold and hungry. It won't happen again," I repeat.

"I don't know what happened, but I really am fine," she says. "Something else is going on. Talk to me."

I look at her. I can't tell this woman how fucked up my head really is. I'm trying to keep her here, not fucking scare her away.

"Louie, you know part of having a girlfriend is having someone you can talk to, someone who will listen without judgement," Charlotte continues.

"I've never had a girlfriend before," I admit.

"Like ever?" she asks.

"I've never wanted anyone to get too close, to see how fucked up I really am," I explain.

"Well, I'm here, and I'm pretty close, so how about you tell me just how fucked up you really are?"

"I can't. I don't want you to run."

"At this point, I'm pretty sure you're some kind of mobster or underworld criminal, and I'm still right here. If that hasn't made me run, what else do you think could?" she asks.

My lips tip up slightly. If only she knew I wasn't

just part of the underworld. I *am* the underworld. "I... My mother was a whore, Charlotte. When I was a kid, she'd leave me in alleyways while she went to work. She always came back for me. Until she didn't. I was there for two days before police found me."

Charlotte stays quiet. She doesn't look at me with disgust or pity. "How old were you?"

"Eight," I tell her. "I have this recurring nightmare of being in that alley. I always wake up starving afterwards."

"Okay," she says.

"Okay?"

"See? Talking? It's okay to talk. I'm still here." Charlotte smiles at me, and I swear I feel some of my tension break off and fall away.

"I wasn't alone in the dream this time..."

"Who was with you?"

"You."

"Me?" she asks.

"You were scared, cold, and hungry. I couldn't keep you safe. I couldn't provide for you." I shake my head, annoyed with myself all over again.

"It wasn't real," Charlotte tells me.

"What if it was? What if one day it is? What if keeping you here is a mistake?"

"Do you feel like this is a mistake?" Charlotte

climbs down from her stool. She swivels mine around and steps between my legs. Her hands land on my bare chest. "Does this feel like a mistake to you, Louie?" she repeats before her lips press against the middle of my chest.

"No," I tell her. "You are not a mistake."

"Louie?"

"Yeah?"

"Take me back to bed," Charlotte says.

Without another word, I stand, pick her up, and carry her back down the hall to the bedroom. My body follows hers onto the mattress. "Coming back to bed is a great idea."

My lips slam onto hers, my body suffering from a different sort of starvation now. I'm hungry for her, more of her, always more. I move my mouth down Charlotte's chin and along her neck.

"You were made to be treasured, sweetheart, but your body... it was made to be fucked," I tell her. My hand slides between us, grazing along her inner thighs. "Fuck, you're dripping. I can feel your wetness all the way down your leg. Is this for me? Are you wet for me?"

Charlotte's hips arch upwards, her core seeking the friction she's desperate for. "I need you," she moans.

"Need, huh? What is it that you need from me?" I ask her.

"I need you to touch me," she says, her breath catching when I do just that. My fingers slide under the piece of lace covering her pussy. Circling around her hard little bud. Her body practically jumps off the bed, her wetness covering my fingers.

"I love how responsive you are," I tell her. "Your body is mine. This is all mine." My teeth bite down on Charlotte's shoulder. I pull my hand back and sit up. Charlotte groans. "I want this off." I tug her shirt —*my shirt*—over her head. Staring at her perfect, C-cup breasts. "These are mine." I cup one and then the other as Charlotte's hands run up and down my chest, my abs.

"Does that make all of this mine?" she asks me.

"It's all yours," I reply as I lean forward, covering her body with mine again.

Charlotte's tongue darts out, licking across my collarbone. "Good, because I licked it, which means it's mine."

I raise a brow at her. "If I lick it, it's mine? Challenge accepted." Taking hold of her wrists, I position her arms above her head. "I'm going to lick you from head to toe. Keep your hands there. Don't move them or I'll tie them up," I warn, and the moan that comes out of her mouth tells me she likes the idea more than I thought she would. "You want to be tied up, sweetheart?"

Charlotte smiles but shakes her head. "I'll be good. I'll keep them here."

"Good girl. Don't move. Your body is a piece of fine art I'm going to take my time exploring." My tongue trails from her shoulder, down to her right breast, before capturing her nipple. I release the hardened bud with a plop before looking up at her. She hasn't moved. "Thank you."

"Why are you thanking me?" Charlotte asks.

"For not running," I tell her before repeating the process with her other nipple.

"Argh, god." Her body moves upwards, and her hands come down on the top of my head.

I smirk around her nipple before letting it go. Fuck, those moans do something to me. They make me feral. I want to record them so I can play them back, over and over. Or better yet, maybe I just need to keep making her come day and night.

Sitting up on my knees, I move her hands back above her head. "Keep them there."

"Sorry." Charlotte giggles. "Continue, please."

"You know, no one else dares to give me orders," I tell her.

"Well, I'm not just anyone," Charlotte says.

"No, you're not." I continue my slow exploration of her body. Licking down her stomach and circling my tongue around her belly button, causing her to squirm and laugh.

When I get to her pussy, I peel her panties down her legs before spreading them wide and lapping at her from bottom to top. "I licked it, so it's mine," I tell Charlotte before diving back in.

Chapter Twenty Four

My arms wrap around Evie's neck. "I can't believe you're here," I choke out, tears threatening to spill free.

She drops her bag to the ground and pulls me closer. "I'm so sorry," she says. "You should never have been alone through any of this."

"Stop! Don't you dare make me cry!" I warn as I

finally release my grip to look my friend up and down.

She's wearing a denim dress. It's fitted, her breasts popping out of the neckline, and she's paired it with white converse high-tops. Sounds casual, but Evie makes even the most-casual outfit look elegant. She's slightly taller than I am, and thinner too. My friend is a beauty queen, like a *legit* beauty queen. She's won pageant after pageant. Her mother forced her into competing until Evie turned twenty and decided to say no more. Her long strawberry-blonde hair hangs in curls down to her waist and her face is perfectly made up.

Evie might have left the pageant world behind, but some habits never *left* her. Like refusing to go out without being perfectly put together. She's just flown across the country, and you wouldn't know it. I glance down at my cutoff denim shorts and the black t-shirt I borrowed from Louie's closet. I look like shit in comparison.

"You look amazing, as always," I tell Evie.

"And you look like you've just had sex." She raises her eyebrows at me. "Oh my god!" She covers her mouth and squeals. "You just had sex."

"Shhh!" I clamp a palm over her face. "I don't

need all of Nevada to hear what a crappy person I am," I tell her.

I drop my hand and Evie shakes her head. "Why on earth would having sex make you a crappy person?"

"Because I was supposed to be married, remember? Runaway bride." I point to myself. "And here I am, shacking up with some guy I just met."

"Yeah, I've seen the man you're shacking up with and he's not just *some guy*." Evie smirks. "He's some insanely hot, tall, dark, sexy, and dangerous guy." Her eyebrows waggle up and down. "Besides, you and Owen were over well before you walked out on the wedding. And we both know it."

She's not wrong. I guess I was in some kind of denial for months, if not a full year before the wedding. "It doesn't matter. I was still engaged not even a week ago."

"Pfft... no one cares," Evie says. "Now, are we going to stand here all day and argue about whether or not you should or should not be having sex, or should we go and stash my bag somewhere and then find a bar?"

"Come on." I grab Evie's suitcase from the ground. And as soon as I do, a man in a suit steps up and takes it from me.

"Miss, Mr. Giuliani sent me to help you with your bags," he says.

"It's one bag," I tell him. "I think we can manage."

"All the same, ma'am, it's my pleasure to help." The guy nods. Turns and starts towards the elevator.

"Talk about service," Evie says, linking her arm with mine. "Guess there are perks to sleeping with the owner."

"Shh." I elbow her in the side. "The orgasms are perks enough, believe me," I tell her quietly.

Once the bellman leaves—after refusing to accept my tip, mind you—I show Evie around before escorting her to the suite where she'll be staying.

"This is nice, like really nice," she says. "Okay, this..." Her hand waves up and down my body. "... isn't going to cut it." She smiles.

"No." I shake my head. I know exactly what she's thinking. She wants to make me over. It's one of her favorite things to do. As much as she hated the pageant world, Evie loved the glam of it.

"Yes," she says with a big smile, while the sound of the door opening has my eyes widening. There is literally only one person who could be walking in right now. Louie.

"Wait here," I tell Evie as I rush towards the

entrance. Only to stop dead in my tracks. *Okay, so maybe there's more than one person who is able to help themselves into this room.* "Babysitting duties again?"

"Something like that. Boss has made reservations for you and your friend at Olives," Sammie tells me.

"Olives?"

"It's a bar downstairs," he says.

"Oh, cool. Tell the boss I said *thanks*." I go to turn back to the room when I run into Evie.

"Hey, I'm Evie, and you are?" She holds out a hand to Sammie.

"Sammie." He takes her palm with a glint in his eye. "Pleasure to meet you."

I look between the two of them before asking, "Where *is* Louie?"

"Ah, he had a meeting," Sammie tells me.

"Okay, well, we're going to be up here for a while. You know, girl stuff. So why don't you go and... I don't know... do what it is you do before you were forced to babysit me," I suggest.

"You have a babysitter?" Evie asks.

I roll my eyes. "Louie seems to think the city isn't safe and that I shouldn't be walking around alone," I explain. "Just pretend he's not here. You'll get used to it. Now, let's do this makeover." I'm hoping my sacrifice of being her personal Barbie doll is going to keep Evie from asking about Louie or his insistent need to give me a bodyguard.

"Yes. Let's do this." Evie drags me back into the bedroom. Her bag gets emptied onto the bed, the contents of which spill out everywhere. I stare at all the makeup, brushes, and clothes. "I've got everything we need. But we should video call Rachel. She shouldn't miss out on this."

"You're right." I smile. "Thank you again for coming here. I didn't know how much I needed you."

"I know. I'm often underrated. But don't stress. I'm here." Evie grins, then it drops. "Seriously, how are you really handling all of this? Have you spoken to Melanie?"

"No, how can I?"

"I don't know, but she's your sister. That's not going away," Evie says.

"She slept with my fiancé. Even if I was going to call it off, Melanie didn't know that and she still slept with Owen. How long were they even going at it behind my back?" I ask.

"I don't know. I *didn't* know. Or I would have told you right after I killed them both and torched their bodies," Evie says with a smile. "There is no murder if there are no bodies, right?"

"Right. I just... She was my best friend. Other than you and Rachel, of course, and I honestly thought nothing could come between us."

"I know." Evie sits on the bed. "I don't know what to say, but I do think you're going to find a way to move on from this somehow. I'm not saying you should forgive her. In fact, I don't think you should. But I do think eventually, for your own sake, you should talk to her."

"Maybe." I shrug as I pick up my phone and hit the video call button next to Rachel's name.

"Hey! I can't believe you're both in Vegas without me," she answers. "But are you okay? I'm really sorry. I know we don't like him right now, but he was a big part of your past."

I look to Evie to see if she has any idea what Rachel is talking about. She shakes her head and lifts a shoulder. I return my focus to my phone. "What are you talking about?" I ask Rachel, positioning the camera so it shows both Evie and me on the screen.

"Ah, Owen. You didn't hear?"

"Hear what?" Evie chimes in.

"Owen is dead," Rachel says, using her well-practiced doctor's tone, "He was found in a hotel room in Vegas. He overdosed."

I blink. He's dead. I blink again. No. Louie

wouldn't have done that. But then his words from last night play over in my head: *I won't ever let anyone hurt you, Charlotte.* Holy shit, Louie killed him.

"Charlotte, are you okay?" Rachel's voice brings me back to the present. "I'm sorry. Of course you're not. That's a stupid question."

"I'm fine. Evie is about to give me a makeover. You wanna watch?" I ask her.

"Ah, sure," Rachel says.

Setting the phone up on the bedside table, I turn to Evie. "Make me as hot as you possibly can."

I want to look good. If I look my best, maybe I'll feel my best—or at the very least better about the fact that I'm sleeping with the person who murdered my ex. And worse than that is the fact that I don't want to stop seeing Louie, even knowing the truth. Or what I'm assuming is the truth...

Chapter Twenty-Five

I've been avoiding Charlotte, not because I don't want to see her. It's because of how fucking much I want to see her. I spilled my guts last night—early this morning. Told her things I've never told anyone, and the fact I did it so easily scares the shit out of me.

What else am I going to spill to this woman? Am

I going to admit that I'm exactly the monster she suspects me of being? Tell her all the ways I break the fucking law? Give her ammunition to use against me? I can't be that goddamn stupid.

I need to remember that as much as I want to keep her, as much as this woman is mine, I can't trust her with all of my shit. I can't trust anyone that much unless they're as knee-deep in it as I am. That's why Carlo, Sammie, and I work so well together.

There's an element of trust between us. Not blind trust. I wouldn't put it past them to stab me in the back. Anyone is capable of that. I don't think they would, but it's a possibility I'm aware of. I watch everyone in my life. Always on the lookout for a traitor, someone trying to take what I've built.

A text notification has me picking up my phone. My thumb swipes at the screen to open the message.

SAMMIE:

Boss, your girl is coming down.
You might wanna take a look.

Take a look? What the fuck is he talking about?
I made sure Charlotte had a table with full service at one of our quieter bars for her to spend time with her friend. Another reason I've been avoiding her is the fact that I don't want to smother

her. Actually, scratch that. I do. I just don't want her to think I'm smothering her.

I pick up the remote to my left and flick through the CCTV until I see her. And fuck, do I see her. A lot of her. "What the fuck is she wearing?"

I'm standing and heading to the door before I realize what I'm doing. I've been holed up in my office all day alone, working through shit that has been piling up since I met Charlotte. Walking through the Casino floor, I don't stop. That is until I see her. Again. This time, in person. I wait for her to look up before making a beeline in her direction.

Her eyes widen, and by the time I reach her, I have my jacket off. "Sweetheart, you look... cold," I tell her, wrapping the fabric around her shoulders as I kiss the middle of her forehead. I look to my friend. He's getting way too much entertainment from me right now. "Carlo is looking for you," I say. He's not. But Sammie doesn't need to know that.

"Right. On it, boss." Sammie shakes his head and walks away.

"Ah, nope, I'm good. Thanks." Charlotte shrugs the jacket off her shoulders and smiles up at me. "Louie, this is Evie. Evie, Louie."

I nod politely at the girl while extending a hand. "Hi, thanks for coming out here to see Charlotte."

Evie takes my palm in hers. "Um, yeah, I've known Charlotte practically my whole life. I think I should be the one thanking you for looking out for her."

"It's not a hardship," I say as I turn back to Charlotte. My eyes take her in. She's wearing a white dress—or is it a shirt? Because I'm pretty sure dresses are supposed to be longer than what she's got on. Sparkly sequins cover the top half of the material, which is hugging her breasts the way my hands ache to. "You look beautiful. Sure you're not cold, though? There isn't a lot of fabric on that shirt."

"It's a dress. And I'm sure. Are you coming to the bar with us?" she asks me.

"I wasn't planning on it, but if you're going out looking like that, I have to come with you to ward off all the assholes who are going to hit on you."

"No one is hitting on me." Charlotte laughs.

"They can hit on me, though, especially that one." Evie nods to her left, and my gaze falls on fucking Emmanuel.

"You don't want to go near *that one*," I reply, while wrapping a possessive arm around Charlotte's waist.

It's not that I think Emanuel would hurt my girl. It's that I don't think *he wouldn't*. If I ever give him a reason to come after me, I know the first thing he'll attack won't be me. It'll be her. That's how his cartel has always worked. He's his father's son after all. I'd be fucking stupid to think otherwise, just because we share a history.

"You okay?" Charlotte looks up at me again, concern written all over her face.

I lean forward and press against the side of her head. "I'm good," I tell her. "Come on, let's get that drink."

"Okay," she says.

"Louie, are you going to introduce me to your friends?" Emmanuel approaches us as we walk towards the bar.

"Emmanuel, this is Charlotte, my girlfriend. And this is Evie," I tell him.

"Well, Charlotte, it's a pleasure to meet the woman who's captured this old bastard's heart," Emmanuel says. He then turns his attention to Evie.

Shit. I know that look. I've seen it on my friend once before. When we were sixteen and he became fixated on a girl named Laura. A girl who looks like she could be sisters with Evie. His obsession lasted a full year until one day the girl disappeared. No one ever saw her again.

"Charlotte, take Evie over to the bar. I'll meet you in there," I say, letting go of her.

"Sure. It was nice to meet you," she says to Emmanuel.

"You too." He nods politely in Charlotte's direction.

I wait until the girls are out of earshot before turning my glare on Emmanuel. "Don't."

"Don't what?" he asks with amusement in his tone.

"I know that look. I've seen it before. Evie isn't her," I remind him.

"Isn't who?"

"Laura," I say her name, and wait for the hit to come. It doesn't. Back when she first disappeared, Emmanuel would swing every time anyone mentioned her. Guess he's developed some self-control over the years.

His jaw twitches. "I don't know who you're talking about," he says, looking me dead in the eye.

"Right, and I'm fucking Father Christmas. Don't fuck with my girl's friend, Emmanuel," I warn him.

"I have no intention of fucking with her. Now, *fucking her*... that's not off the table." He smirks and turns around, heading in the girls' direction.

I pull out my phone and text the guys. I'm not

dealing with the fallout of Emmanuel's fucked-up mind.

> **ME:**
> Come and rein in E. He's got the Laura look for Charlotte's friend.

> **SAMMIE:**
> Saw that one coming. She looks like her ghost.

> **CARLO:**
> This I gotta see. Nothing unravels that bastard.

> **ME:**
> This is Charlotte's friend. She cannot get mixed up with E. Get here, now.

> **SAMMIE:**
> On it. Although you did just send me away.

Pocketing my phone, I make my way over to the table I haven't taken my eyes off. Emmanuel is sitting next to Evie and Charlotte—whose eyes are on me. I sit down and drag her chair over until it's pressed up against mine. My arm wraps around the back. "How was your day?" I ask Charlotte.

"I was Evie's personal Barbie doll, so *hell*," she whispers.

"I heard that you loved every minute of my abuse." Evie waves an accusatory finger at her friend.

"Sure I did." Charlotte laughs.

"So, Louie, tell me. How'd you do it?" Evie asks me.

"Do what?"

"How'd you kill Charlotte's ex and make it look like an overdose?" she clarifies, her eyes fixed on my face. My expression.

I blink at her. And then look to Charlotte, who is staring back at me, waiting for my answer.

"He didn't," Emmanuel says. "I did."

"Do you just go around killing all of your friends' girlfriends' exes?" Evie raises a curious brow at him.

"Only the ones who leave bruises on my friend's girlfriends," Emmanuel replies without missing a beat.

"So, are you like an assassin or something?" Evie tilts her head to the side.

I can't get a read on this chick. *Is she serious right now? Or does she think this is all a joke?*

"No, but ever heard of the De La Sangre Cartel?" Emmanuel asks.

"Fucking hell," I groan.

Evie ignores me. "No, should I have?"

"Probably best you haven't. I run the organization," Emmanuel tells her.

"Emmanuel, really?" I grunt.

"So, you're supposed to be a big scary drug lord or something?" Evie continues to probe. "I don't see it. You don't look that scary."

"He's full of shit. That's why. We didn't kill Owen," I tell her, annoyed that I'm lying to Charlotte without having much of a choice but to do it. "What happened?"

"Rachel said he was found in a hotel room. Overdosed. But it's strange... I mean, I know the guy was an asshole, but he didn't do drugs. He wasn't an addict," Charlotte says.

"We also didn't think he was *doing* sisters but he did that too." Evie shrugs. "I say good riddance. The asshole broke your heart. I just wish I could have been the one to end him. I even bought a shovel."

"He didn't break my heart," Charlotte says. "My sister did."

"Semantics. So, tell me more about this cartel of yours. What exactly do you do other than kill people?" Evie returns her focus to Emmanuel.

"You hungry? Let's order food," I interject, before my idiot friend can say anything more. I'm pretty sure Evie thinks he's joking at this point, but you can never be too sure. Or careful.

Chapter Twenty-Six

My girls' night with Evie has turned into us two girls surrounded by Louie's friends. About ten minutes after Louie sat down with us, Sammie and Carlo turned up. Not to mention all the guys standing nearby in black suits, who haven't moved an inch since we took our seats. I don't know who they are, but they're watching our table.

I've been listening to Evie flirt with Louie's friend Emmanuel, and he is eating it up, telling her all about his home in Mexico. At first, I thought he was joking. Now, I'm not so sure.

I lean towards Louie and whisper, "He's not joking, is he? He actually runs a cartel?"

Louie stiffens. His hand wraps around the nape of my neck and his lips press against my ear. "Let's just say I wouldn't leave you in a room alone with him."

"Okay. Evie, I want to dance." I stand and reach for her hand. There's a small dance floor towards the front of the bar. No one is on it, but right now, I don't care. I need to get her away from Louie's *friend*.

I drag Evie towards the dance floor, and it takes less than thirty seconds for half of the men standing around in suits to follow us.

"I don't think that guy is joking about owning a cartel," I tell her as I wrap my arms around her neck, being sure to lower my voice so no one else can hear us.

"I don't think he is either." She laughs.

"Stop flirting with him, Evie!"

"Why? A man like that knows how to fuck,

Charlotte." She laughs again. We haven't had enough alcohol to be drunk yet, but we are both definitely tipsy.

"This isn't a joke. I don't want anything to happen to you." I pull her closer, rubbing my body up against hers as we dance.

"So, you're the only one who gets to jump into bed with a dangerous man? It's just sex. I'll be fine."

"Wait... You're already planning on spending the night with him?" I ask her.

"No, I'm planning on spending a hot few hours with the man and then never seeing him again." She smiles before her eyes dart behind me. "Incoming."

I turn my head and see Louie walking up to us, a frown on his face. "Can I cut in?" he asks Evie.

"Be my guest," she replies.

Louie wraps an arm around my waist and pulls me towards him. "I don't like you rubbing up against other people," he grunts.

"She's my friend. Don't worry. I'm not into girls." I laugh at him.

"Still don't like it," he says.

"Anyone ever tell you that you have a serious jealous streak?"

"I've never had a reason to be jealous before, so no," he says.

"Okay then." I grin.

After dancing to one more song, I drag Louie back to the table. I can feel the alcohol wearing off. I need another drink.

"What the fuck are you all looking at?" Louie grunts, meeting the glare of everyone currently staring in our direction.

"Were you just dancing?" Carlo asks with a smile on his lips.

Louie lifts a brow. "So?"

"You don't dance," Sammie says.

"Well, there was that one time. In junior high. School dance. He danced with someone then. Who was she?" Emmanuel shakes his head. "Doesn't matter. Point is, there was the one time."

"Should I be jealous? You danced with someone else once in your life?" I ask Louie.

"No," he tells me.

"Don't worry. Charlotte isn't the jealous type," Evie says.

"Really?" Sammie doesn't seem convinced.

I shake my head. "I'm really not."

"Huh, maybe we should take a walk. Let's go visit another bar," Carlo suggests.

"Yes, let's." Evie and I jump up at the same time.

"This will be fun," Sammie murmurs.

"So much," Carlo agrees with him.

Louie stands. His hand wraps firmly around mine, and he pulls me against his side. "Stick close to me," he says into my ear.

"Why? Scared I'm going to disappear?" I ask him.

"Yes," he replies, his tone serious.

"I'm probably not." I laugh at him.

We end up following Carlo and Sammie through the casino floor. A lot of people stop and talk to Louie, who never lets go of my hand. His grip tightens on me as we enter a section marked: *high rollers*. He seems tense. Then again, he's always tense when other people are around.

When it's just us, locked in the confines of his apartment, that's when he's more relaxed. He opened up to me last night, about his childhood and his nightmares. I wanted to hug him. Hold him tight and tell him that he wasn't going to be alone ever again. That I'd stay as long as he wanted me to stay.

I didn't do any of that. Because I'm not trying to come across as a clinger. Also, my head is urging me to slow the hell down. I just don't know how. I'm so caught in this man's web and there doesn't seem to be a way out. Not that I've really looked for one.

A woman, who's definitely more like a goddess,

walks towards us with a huge smile on her cherry-painted lips. Her eyes are directly on Louie when she reaches us—or I should say *him*—because she doesn't even look in my direction. Her hand lands on his chest and her red mouth presses against his cheek.

"Louie, darling, I was hoping to see you tonight." Her French accent sends shivers through me.

Louie tightens his hold on my hand as I'm attempting to pry myself free. I want nothing more than to shrink into the background. "Julie, this is my girlfriend, Charlotte," he says, looking down at me.

I smile at the woman, even though it's the last thing I want to do. "Hello," I say, using my sweetest southern voice. Her hand doesn't leave Louie's chest, not until he reaches up and physically removes it.

"How nice," Julie directs to me, then turns back to Louie. "I'm in my usual room. When you're done playing house, come and find me."

"Oh, sweetheart, you clearly ain't got any of the good sense God gave a rock because you are so barking up the wrong tree right now," Evie tells her.

"Who are you? And why are you here?" Julie snarls while waving a hand at Evie. And I see it right before it lands. *It* being the glass of champagne that comes up and splashes all over the front of my friend's dress.

Evie doesn't budge. "Bless your heart. You think a spilled drink is going to bother me?"

Before the woman can answer, Evie is being hauled backwards while two men in black suits come up behind Julie, grabbing her by the arms. "Miss, it's time to leave," one of them says in a thick Mexican accent.

"Emmanuel, no." Louie's voice is low but I hear it. *Does he want this woman to stay? Why?* "She's the daughter of the French president."

Emmanuel says something in Spanish to the two men and they disappear with Julie.

"A friend of yours?" I ask Louie.

"The daughter of a friend," he tells me.

"I take it back."

"You take what back?" Louie looks at me, his brows drawn down.

"I think I do get jealous," I whisper.

He smiles. Wide. "That's not a bad thing. It means you care." He shrugs before adding, "And just so you know, you have no reason to be jealous."

I snort. "Yeah, no reason to be jealous of some gorgeous French model. No reason at all."

"Keep an eye on those two," he tells Carlo,

nodding his head at Evie and Emmanuel, who are looking way too cozy. Then Louie drags me away.

"Where are we going?" I ask him.

"My office is just through here," he says.

"Why are we going to your office?"

"Because I need to prove to you just how much you don't have anything to worry about. I've never wanted to fuck Julie, Charlotte. But you... There hasn't been a minute that's past since I first saw you that I haven't wanted to fuck you."

"Oh." *Well, shit. I could be down for that.* "No. Wait." I dig my feet into the carpet.

"What's wrong?"

"We can't. I can't leave Evie. This was supposed to be our girls' night. Can I get a rain check on the *you fucking me* thing?" As much as I want to go to Louie's office with him, I can't abandon my friend.

"Okay." Louie adjusts himself in his pants. "Just keep in mind... I've been hard since the moment I saw you tonight."

"I know." I smile. I saw the bulge in his pants, and it's not like I'm not just as eager for him. I am. But I want to be a good friend too.

Louie leads us back over to the group. "Let's drink," he says, guiding everyone towards wherever it is we're going.

A few minutes later, we end up in a very lush-looking bar. Where I slide into a booth until I'm squished between Evie and Louie. "You know, he's a little intense," she whispers to me.

"Who?"

"Louie. He doesn't stop fussing over you," she says.

"I know." I smile. "It's... different."

"Good. You deserve that," she tells me.

"Truth or dare?" Carlo says from the other side of the table.

"What are we? In middle school?" Louie groans.

"Truth," I say.

"Okay, Charlotte. Brave girl going first. Truth, it is. Are you secretly obsessed with me and using Louie here as a way to get close to me, 'cause I could be open to that." Carlo laughs.

"Absolutely not," I tell him. "But don't worry. I'm sure there's a girl out there somewhere for you."

"Dare," Evie chimes in.

"I dare you to go hit on that guy and get his number." Sammie points to a man standing at the bar —again, in a black-on-black suit.

Evie smiles. "*Please*, that's like taking candy from a baby." She literally climbs up onto the table to get out of the booth.

We all watch her approach the guy. "I'm going to slaughter him like a pig," Emmanuel mutters under his breath, although I hear it loud and clear.

Evie returns a few minutes later with a confused look on her face. "He's gay," she says.

"No, he's not." Sammie laughs. "He just wants to keep his head on his shoulders."

"Nope, he's gay. That's never happened to me before. Shit. Am I... Oh my god!" Evie shrieks.

"What?" I ask as she climbs back over the table to plop down next to me.

"I'm losing it. I'm getting... old."

"You are not losing it," I tell her before changing the subject. "Okay, dare."

"I've got this one," Louie interjects. Then he leans in and whispers in my ear. "I dare you to marry me. Tonight."

Chapter Twenty-Seven

Louie

Holy fuck, *did I really just dare Charlotte to marry me?* I did, and I'm not taking it back either. Don't get me wrong. I'm not going to force her to go along with my craziness, but I also won't stop her if she does.

Charlotte's eyes widen. Her mouth drops open. "I'm terrified you're actually serious."

I lift a shoulder. "What's it going to be? Yes or no? It's a simple dare," I tell her.

"Simple? How many times have you done this before?" she asks me.

"Never."

"Me either. Not so simple."

"When it's you, I feel like it's very simple. I'm game if you are." I won't lie. My heart is beating out of my chest as I wait for her response.

"Okay, sure. Let's do it," she says.

I look at her. She just said yes. "Let's go before you change your mind." I stand and hold a hand out to Charlotte before turning to the rest of the group. "We're getting married."

"You're *what* now?" Sammie and Carlo blurt at the same time.

"Ah, Charlotte, how drunk are you?" Evie asks.

"A little. But it's fine. It's Louie." Charlotte smiles and leans her body against mine. My arm wraps around her waist.

"Charlotte, this isn't pretend. This is real." Evie jumps to her feet.

"I know," Charlotte responds, while I'm mentally reminding myself that I cannot get rid of her friend. But if Evie talks sense into Charlotte, I might just be pissed enough to do it.

It's a fluke that she's even going along with the idea. I'm not taking any chances that she'll change her mind. I'm also ignoring how much I actually want this. I barely know this woman. I mean, I know everything I need to know after looking her up, but we've also *known* each other for a couple of days.

My gut is telling me to do whatever it takes to keep her, and if marrying her is what achieves that, then I'm marrying her. I've never felt the need to keep a woman close. I've never wanted anyone the way I want Charlotte, which is why I'm doing what has to be done.

"Okay, well, at least I get to be your bridesmaid," Evie says. "And you're wearing white."

"Because I'm totally a virgin bride," Charlotte deadpans.

"You are in some places," I say, quietly, so only she can hear me. Her face goes red. "For now."

"Okay, you're actually doing this? Let me call someone." Sammie shakes his head while taking his phone out of his pocket. "Carlo, get the cars. We're going to the Little White Chapel."

"Are you really sure? You can change your mind. I won't be offended." Charlotte turns to me. Her hands rest on my chest. I grab hold of them.

"I don't think I've ever been more sure of

anything before. I want you to be mine, Charlotte. Really mine."

"Okay."

***

"This is legally binding," the guy dressed as Elvis tells me with a look of fear on his face.

"I would hope so," I grunt at him. "We're getting married."

"Right, of course, sir." He nods. "Stand up here." He looks to Charlotte and then to me again. "Do you have your own vows, or do you want to recite the standard ones?"

"I have my own," Charlotte says.

"Okay, Miss Armstrong, you can go first. Please, face each other and hold hands."

Charlotte locks her fingers around mine. Her smile is wide. "Louie, I believe people come into our lives when we need them the most. The night we met, I needed you more than you think. We haven't known each other long, but I do feel like I've known you all my life. I promise to support you in your endeavors. I promise to always be there—in sickness and health, richer or poorer. I promise to be yours and only yours. I promise to never leave you alone."

I suck in a breath. She knows my biggest fear, the nightmare that haunts me. "Charlotte, you are the light I didn't know I needed in my life. You have given me a reason to be a better person. I promise to always put you first, to make your happiness and well-being my top priority. I promise to be faithful to you always. I am yours."

I don't hear what *Elvis* says next. I'm so focused on Charlotte until I hear the words: "You may kiss the bride."

My arms wrap around her waist and I pick her up off the ground as my lips slam onto hers. My tongue delves into her mouth, fighting for dominance when the realization hits me. She's my wife. I'm kissing my wife.

"We did it," Charlotte says when I pull back to look at her. "Are we insane?"

"Probably, but at least we can be insane together."

"Oh my god!" I hear the scream coming from the phone Evie has flipped in our direction. "Charlotte, what the hell? You got married without me?"

"Sorry, Rach, couldn't wait." Charlotte laughs.

"Ah, Rachel, I'll call you back later." Evie drops the phone back in her bag before she steals my wife from me, pulling her friend into a tight hug. "I'm really sorry, Charlotte. I'm crashing."

"Okay, we'll go back to the hotel," Charlotte tells her. "Are you okay?"

Evie nods. But she looks a little... I don't know what it is... Weak?

Charlotte looks to me. "I have to get her back to the room."

"What's wrong with her?" I ask.

"She just needs to sleep. She'll be fine."

"Okay, let's go." I take hold of Charlotte's hand. She has Evie's in her other, and I don't miss the way she keeps looking at her friend with concern.

Sammie and Carlo climb into the second car, while Emmanuel climbs into the front of ours.

Before we get back to the Royal Flush, Evie is asleep. "You might wanna wake her up," I tell Charlotte. "We're almost there."

"I can't. She won't wake up for a while now."

"What do you mean?" This comes from Emmanuel, who turns to look at Evie. I don't know what his deal is, but he needs to get a hold of himself. This girl is not for him.

"She has insomnia. She stays awake for days at a time, and then she'll just crash and sleep for hours without getting up," Charlotte explains. "We won't be able to wake her."

"It's okay." Emmanuel gets out of the car as soon as it stops in front of the casino. "I've got her," he says, opening the back door and scooping Evie into his arms.

"Are you sure?" Charlotte asks.

He nods. "Lead the way. Where is her room?"

I take everyone over to the staff elevator to save the trip through the casino floor. After leaving Evie in bed, I tell Emmanuel I'll catch up with him tomorrow and wait for the elevator to close. It was obvious he didn't want to leave Evie alone. But Charlotte assured him that she'd be asleep for at least sixteen hours.

I guide Charlotte into my penthouse. I guess it's *our* penthouse now. "Shit, I did it wrong," I say, opening the door again. "Redo."

I take her back to the other side of the door and pick her up. She squeals. "What are you doing?"

"Carrying my wife over the threshold." I smile.

"Oh." Once we're inside again, I lock the door and carry Charlotte into the bedroom. I've been waiting all fucking night to get this dress off her.

"Say it again," she whispers.

"Say what?"

"Your wife," she tells me.

"You, Mrs. Giuliani, are my wife. Mine."

"I think I like being your wife already." She giggles.

"Good, because forever would be a long time to not like it." I toss Charlotte onto the bed. She lands in the middle of the king-size mattress, and her hair fans out around her like a halo. "I think you might actually be an angel."

"I'm not." She laughs.

"Agree to disagree." I climb onto the bed and lie next to her. Charlotte turns her face towards mine, and my hand cups her cheek. "I love you." My words are soft, barely a whisper.

"I... I feel like I'm falling in love with you more and more every minute," Charlotte says.

"I'm going to make sure you never have a reason to stop falling," I tell her while praying that I can actually deliver on that promise.

Chapter Twenty-Eight

Mrs. Giuliani. That's me. I'm her. I really married Louie, a man who is basically a stranger.

Sure, I know what his touch feels like. I know that I am falling in love with him. But marriage? It's insane, and yet I couldn't think of a single reason not to be with him. To be his.

There is that whole he killed my ex thing, though. Not that he's confirmed it. He doesn't have to, because I don't for an instance think he didn't do it. And still, I find myself not wanting to be anywhere else but right here. In bed with him.

"Louie?"

"Yeah?"

"What really happened to Owen?" I ask.

Louie's hand, which was caressing up and down my arm, suddenly stills. "I can't tell you that, Charlotte."

"I'm supposed to be your wife. If you can't tell me things, how is a marriage between us going to work?"

"There is no *supposed to be*. You *are* my wife," he says. "And I already told you I made sure he can't hurt you again."

"I don't want you to do anything that will get you in trouble."

Louie smiles. "I'm not planning on getting into any sort of trouble."

"I also don't know how I feel about it all. Owen being dead, I mean. I know what he did was horrible, but there was a time I thought I was going to spend the rest of my life with him. We were happy once. I might not have been in love with him. I know that now. But he wasn't always a bad person either."

"Charlotte?"

"Yeah?"

"I'm more than happy to talk about your ex with you... to help you work through whatever it is you're feeling. But, let's not talk about other men. Here. Now. The only people I want in this bed are you and me," Louie says. "I want you completely. I get that you have a past with someone else, but I have your future."

"You do." I smile at my husband, then quickly shoot up in bed. "Holy shit."

"What?" Louie props himself on an arm, his eyes roaming over every inch of my body like he's looking for some invisible injury.

"You're my husband." I smile wider.

Louie's features soften. "I am."

"Hearts are going to break all over the strip as soon as people know you're married," I tell him. "I've seen the way women look at you." I don't like it either. This jealousy thing is new for me.

"Want me to tattoo it across my forehead? Property of Charlotte?" he asks.

"Not your forehead, no." I laugh. My hands land on his chest, pushing him backwards before I straddle his hips. "But you are mine, which means all of this..." My fingers dance across the buttons of his shirt. "... is mine too."

"All yours," Louie repeats. His hips shift upwards, his hard cock grinding against my core. Then he sits up and reaches for something on the nightstand. "But hold that thought. I forgot to show you something."

"What is it?" I ask when he hands me his phone.

"Our test results. Well, most of 'em. Doc said some shit's pending. But so far, so good. We're both clean as a whistle."

"I'm clean. I know I am and I trust that you are." I discard his phone, tossing it to the side of the bed.

"Does that mean we can forgo the condoms now?" Louie questions.

"As soon as I get on birth control, absolutely," I tell him. I can't just throw away all my good sense. Even if most of it has gone out the window with this man.

"I'll set up an appointment tomorrow," he says, his hands traveling higher along my bare thighs.

"Do you believe in love at first sight?"

"I do now," he tells me.

"Me too." I smile.

I thought it was just lust. I mean, when you look

at this man... Six-foot-three, all muscle—like every inch of him is hard. Tan skin, dark hair, the five o'clock shadow on his chiseled jaw, and those eyes that penetrate straight through to my soul. Yeah, how could you not lust after him? But now, I know it's more.

I lean forward, my lips a breath away from his. "Louie?"

"Mmm?"

"I think we should make this marriage official. Consummate it," I tell him.

"I think that's the best idea you've had since you said *yes* to marrying me." He flips us over so I'm on my back again.

My wetness coats my inner thighs. I'm so turned on right now, so ready for him. I've always liked sex. But sex with Louie? I love it. I need it. He makes me feel like no one else ever has.

His hands slip underneath my ass, cupping my cheeks. "Fuck, I love your ass. Mine. I should tattoo my name all over it," he says, as his fingers hook under the edge of my panties. He pulls them down my legs before tossing them over a shoulder.

Then he shrugs out of his shirt before he undoes his pants, freeing his cock. I can never stop staring at it. It's fucking huge. I'm surprised it even fits, to be honest. But his size is also the reason my vagina is so sore afterwards. That and the way Louie fucks me as if he's a starved animal and I'm his last meal.

"I can't wait any longer. I need to be in you now, Charlotte."

"Then don't wait."

Louie reaches into the nightstand and pulls out a condom. I know he doesn't want to use it, but I appreciate that he does it anyway. The moment he's sheathed, he lines up his cock with my entrance and slams into me. Bottoming out.

"Oh, shit!" I yell, the slight sting a welcomed pain I've become accustomed to over the last few days.

"Fuck! Charlotte, I swear it gets better and better," he says, slowly withdrawing from me. "Mine, you are mine." He slams into me again. "This pussy is mine." He pulls out and drives right back in before he leans forward and places a kiss on the middle of my chest. "Your heart is mine." Moving upwards, he kisses my forehead this time. "Your everything is mine."

I can feel my pussy protesting, clinging, convulsing around his cock as he draws back again. There's not one cell of my body that doesn't want to be owned by this man. Maybe I should tattoo his name all over me. Because, let's face it, that wouldn't be the craziest thing I've done this week.

All thoughts vanish when Louie pushes back inside me, bottoming out while he lifts my hips off the mattress. Angling my body so that the tip of his cock hits that spot so deep only he's managed to find it.

Louie shifts onto his knees. Picking up my legs and resting them on his shoulders. His lips press against my inner ankle as he continues to slowly, ever so torturously, slide in and out of me.

The sensations flowing through my every nerve ending are intense, almost unbearable. "Please," I cry out. I need more. I need him to move faster.

"Please what, Mrs. Giuliani?"

"I need more..." *More of what? I have no fucking idea.*

"I know what you need. I've got everything you need right here," Louie says, as if he can somehow read my thoughts. He starts thrusting into me harder, faster.

It only takes minutes before my mind goes blank and I'm seeing stars. "Holy fuck!" I yell, and my body spasms as wave after wave of pleasure runs through me.

"Fuck, I love when you come. Your pussy milks

my cock so fucking good. Just like that. It's all yours, Charlotte." Louie grunts as his thrusts become more rigid, and then he stills. Slowly pulling out of me and collapsing next to me on the bed. "I'm so fucking glad we get a lifetime of doing this," he pants.

"Mmm, me too." I smile, my eyes closed as exhaustion creeps in.

Who on earth is yelling? I open my eyes. The room is dark, and I'm alone. Again. You'd think the morning after I got married I'd at least wake up with my husband in bed with me.

I jolt upwards. "Holy shit, I got married." My eyes widen at the realization of what happened last night. I wasn't drunk. I *was* tipsy, sure, but not drunk. No, I married Louie on a dare because I wanted to. No other reason.

"Wake her up!" someone shouts.

"I'm not waking up my wife for you." *This* comes from Louie.

I feel a smile spread across my face. He just

called me *his wife*. Why does that one little phrase send butterflies fluttering through my stomach?

I climb out of bed, walk into Louie's closet, and pull on a shirt. I then grab a pair of his sweats. Once I'm satisfied I don't look like shit, I walk out to the living room, where Louie and Emmanuel are in a heated conversation.

I shriek when I spot the gun aimed at my husband's head, and Louie calls out over a shoulder. Calmly. A little too calmly. "Charlotte, go back to the bedroom."

"Don't move," Emmanuel says, dropping the gun and turning his attention to me. "Something is wrong with Evie."

"What? What happened?" I'm already walking towards the door.

"She's talking in her sleep. I want to know what happened to her. Who the fuck is she talking about?" Emmanuel asks.

I stop. Dead in my tracks. "She's probably having a nightmare. She has them from time to time. They're not real," I lie.

There *is* a reason for Evie's insomnia, but her secrets are just that. Hers. I'm not going to be the one to tell this maniac. Until something occurs to me and I aim my glare on Emmanuel.

"How do you know she's talking in her sleep?" I ask him.

"I was watching her," he says, pointing a finger in my direction. "And you're lying to me."

Louie steps between us. "Don't fucking speak to her like that," he growls.

"I'm going to find out. You might as well tell me, Charlotte. Someone did something to her, and I want to know who it was," Emmanuel says.

"I think that's something you should ask her. When she's awake," I tell him. "But don't expect her to open up to you. She doesn't talk about her past."

The only reason I know about it is because we got drunk once and she let it slip. The nightmare that Evie has lived isn't one I would wish on my worst enemy.

Then again, if I tell Emmanuel, would he seek his own sort of justice for her?

"But say they were real... If you could find the person who caused those nightmares, what would you do about it?" I ask him. I would never betray my friend's trust, but maybe knowing her real-life version of the boogeyman was gone would help her move on?

"You don't want to know what I'll do, because those are the kind of nightmares that will keep *you* awake at night." Emmanuel smiles, like he'd enjoy whatever it is he's imagining.

"Look, I don't know the full story, because like I said, she doesn't talk about it. But I'm sure if you dug into the pageant world, you'd find the reason behind her nightmares. That's all I'm saying," I tell him. "Anything else you want to know, you'll have to ask Evie."

"Thank you." Emmanuel nods. "I will ask her. When do you think she'll wake up?"

"I have no idea." I shrug and watch as he walks out of the penthouse. I look to Louie. "Are you okay?"

"Am I okay?" He turns to me, his face hard as stone. "I asked you to go back to the bedroom, Charlotte. There was a literal madman waving a gun around in here."

"That madman is your friend, and he wasn't pointing it at me," I explain. "He was pointing it at you."

"That's because he knows if he'd directed it at you, I would have shoved barrel up his ass before pulling the trigger." Louie walks past me, through to the kitchen.

I follow him, about to respond, when we're interrupted by another one of his lunatic friends barging in.

"Louie, SOS!" Carlo yells out through the penthouse.

"Kitchen," Louie yells back, then gestures to me. "Sit. You need to eat."

"First of all, I'm not a dog. You can't just say *sit* and expect me to follow orders," I tell him. "Second, I am starving, so thank you." I reluctantly lower myself onto the stool.

Louie stares at me, a bewildered look on his face. "I love you," he says at the same time Carlo walks into the kitchen. Except he's not alone. He has a child with him. A little girl. I didn't know Carlo had a little girl.

Louie looks at the girl and then up at his friend. "For the love of god, tell me you did not steal someone's kid."

Chapter Twenty-Nine

Louie

Of all the shit I'd expect Carlo to bring to my doorstep, a child is the last thing on that long-ass list.

"He didn't steal me. He's my daddy," the kid says.

I blink. "He's what now?" I direct my confusion to Carlo.

"She, ah, was dropped off with a note," he says.

I walk around the counter and bend so I'm at the little girl's height. "Hi, I'm Louie. What's your name, sweetheart?"

"My name's Jazzy. It's short for Jasmine, like the princess," she says.

"Well, Jazzy, it's nice to meet you. Why don't you sit up here? I'm about to make breakfast." I pick her up and sit her on a stool next to Charlotte. "This is my wife, Charlotte."

"Hi, you're very pretty," Jazzy comments.

"Thank you. So are you, sweetie," Charlotte replies.

I grab a bowl of precut fruit salad from the fridge and place it in front of the girls. "I have some paperwork for Carlo. I forgot to give it to him yesterday," I tell Charlotte. "Be right back."

I kiss her cheek before walking out of the kitchen with my very-silent friend following me. Once we're closed inside the office, I turn to Carlo.

"What the fuck?"

"I don't know, man. She was left at reception with a note." He pulls a piece of paper from his pocket. "I freaked. I didn't know what to do."

I snatch the note from his hand, read it, and give it back. "First, you need a DNA test. She might not even be yours. Second, if she is yours, then I guess we have a new addition to the family." I shrug.

"I don't know the first thing about kids. Or being a father." Carlo scratches his head.

"I don't think there's a manual. Just... feed her, keep her clean and safe. It can't be that hard," I tell him.

"Right. I can do that." Carlo nods in agreement. "She's tiny. How hard can it be?"

"Exactly," I say. "What does she know about her mother?"

"I don't know," he says. "I came straight here."

"Ask her. Find out whatever you can, so we can track the woman down," I tell him.

When I walk back out to the kitchen, Charlotte is at the stove. The smell of bacon fills the air.

I close my arms around her waist and tug her back to my chest. "You don't need to do that."

"I like cooking, and I know you need to eat," she says. "Is it always this... busy around here?"

"No," I tell her. "I'll revoke everyone's access to this floor."

"Don't do that. They're your friends. But seriously, did Carlo really not know he had a daughter?" she whispers.

"He wouldn't abandon a kid he knew about."

None of us would. We might not know how to be parents, but we sure as shit know what *not* to do.

"What's he gonna do?" Charlotte asks.

I glance over my shoulder. Where Carlo is sitting next to Jazzy, a look of wonder on his face. "I think he's going to be fine. You know, once the shock wears off."

Charlotte nods before adding, "I need to go and check on Evie."

"I'll come with you after we eat," I tell her.

Carlo took Jazzy to his penthouse at Aces High. He looked like he was on the verge of a panic attack, but I know he's going to do the right thing by this kid. We're all products of shitty parents. If I thought for one minute that little girl wasn't safe or her well-being wasn't going to become my friend's top priority, I would have made him leave her here. I will never be the person who sits by and lets a child become a victim.

Charlotte is waiting in the living room when I

walk out. She smiles, then pinches her arm. "Ouch." She frowns.

My steps quicken as I approach her. I pick up her arm and bring it to my mouth, kissing over the small red mark she left there. "Why would you hurt yourself?"

"I was checking if I was dreaming, or if this is really my life now. How are you my husband? Have you seen yourself? I mean, I've never won anything before, but I feel like I might have won the husband lottery."

"That's not true. You won a room upgrade just last week." I chuckle. "And I'm the one winning here, sweetheart. I get to keep you." My arm snakes around her back and I pull her against me.

"Mmm, well, you won't have me if Evie wakes up to a strange man in her room and I'm not there. Because she *will* kill me," Charlotte says, pulling away.

"I don't care who they are. If someone tries to hurt you, you can believe I will kill them first," I grunt.

"It's a figure of speech, Louie. She wouldn't actually kill me." Charlotte frowns again. "You really need to not take everything so seriously."

"Your safety is a *serious* matter." I grab her hand.

kylie Kent

"Come on, I'll drag Emmanuel out of there if I have to."

"He wouldn't hurt her, would he?" Charlotte asks me.

I can't lie to this woman, but I also don't want to make her worry. "I think his fascination with her is a little odd. But I don't think he'd hurt her." *At least not yet.*

Charlotte sighs. "Yeah, I didn't get that vibe from him. He seems like he really likes her, almost like he knows her from somewhere else," she says. "Maybe they're star-crossed lovers from a past life."

"This isn't a movie or a book where everyone gets a happily ever after. Trust no one, Charlotte."

"What about you? Should I trust you?" She lifts a brow in my direction.

"Trust no one but me," I clarify.

"Who do you trust? You can't go through life without trusting anyone, Louie," she says.

"Trusting no one is the reason I've gotten to where I am, Charlotte. Trusting people only leads you to being blind when they stab you in the back. Or in my world, in the front."

"That's really sad. I hope that one day you'll learn to trust me," she says.

"I married you, Charlotte. I wouldn't have done that if I didn't trust you."

"But you just said..."

"I know what I said. You aren't just anyone. You're my wife." I lean down and kiss her before adding, "Which also means you can't testify against me."

Charlotte's eyes widen. "Why would I testify against you?"

"You can't. Married, remember? And it was a joke. Relax. I'm not stupid enough to get caught." I open the door to the other penthouse suite, walking in before Charlotte. I want to make sure none of Emmanuel's goons are lurking around. It's empty, so I follow Charlotte down the small hall to the bedroom where her friend is still sleeping.

Sure enough, just as I expected, Emmanuel is sitting in the corner of the bedroom. Just staring at the motionless form on the bed. "Let's go," I tell him.

"Since when do I take orders from you?" He cocks his head to the side.

"Since I just doubled my imports and we have shit to discuss," I remind him, before turning to Charlotte. "I'll be downstairs in my office if you need anything."

"I'll be fine," she says.

Emmanuel follows me out. "What's the real reason you wanted me out of that room?" he asks when the door clicks closed.

"My wife is in there and I don't particularly trust you around her," I tell him.

"You need to learn to trust people. I have no intentions of doing anything to your wife," he says. "Also, can we admit it's fucking weird as shit that you even have a wife?"

"It's a change." I shrug. "What are you doing with Evie? You do know she's not Laura."

"I know," he grunts. "Because Laura's been dead for seven years."

I suspected as much.

"Don't hurt her," I warn him. The last thing I need is to have to explain to Charlotte why her friend is missing. There's also the thought of her being upset that doesn't sit well with me. "I need to buy a ring."

"What?"

"I need to buy Charlotte a ring. She doesn't have one and I don't want her walking around here looking single," I tell Emmanuel.

"It doesn't matter if she has a ring. Your wife is a ten, Louie. Assholes are still gonna try to hit on her.

And this desert ain't big enough to bury them all."
He laughs.

"I'll burn them then," I groan. "Oh, and Carlo
has a kid."

Emmanuel stops dead in his tracks. "What?
Since when?"

"Since this morning. Someone dumped a little
girl at reception. Came with a letter telling him she's
his," I explain.

"Who's the mother?"

"No idea. There was no name," I say.

*At least she cared enough about the kid to leave
her with people, and not in a dark alley between two
dumpsters.* That thought, I keep to myself.

Chapter Thirty

Charlotte

I manage to shower, dress, put on a bit of makeup, and blow dry my hair before Evie wakes up. I'm kinda glad, because I feel like I needed some alone time to wrap my head around the fact that I just got married. And not just to anyone. To Louie. The man looks like he's just stepped off a runway all the damn time. When he came out of the room this morning dressed in a three-piece suit, I thought I was dreaming.

How is that man my husband?

Then there's the whole "I'll kill anyone who hurts you" thing I am working through on my own. Mostly, I'm just trying to accept that it's okay for me to *accept* him for who he is. There's a part of me that says I need to object to his less than law-abiding way of life. When it comes down to it, I don't, though. I really am falling in love with him, despite his morally gray nature. Or is it because of it?

I'm not sure. But when I'm with Louie, I feel like I'm myself for the first time in a long time. He's not trying to make me into the version of me he wants me to be. Which is exactly what it was like with Owen. Who I really can't think about right now. If I do, guilt overwhelms me. He's dead because of me. There is no getting around that.

I wonder how my sister is handling it? Is she heartbroken? Do I care? *Yes, I would never want my sister to feel heartbreak.*

"Hey, you look nice," Evie says as she sleepily makes her way into the living room.

"I've been waiting for you to wake up," I tell her.

"Let me get coffee first," she groans and walks into the small kitchen area.

I stand and throw my phone onto the table. I was contemplating reaching out to my sister. Or maybe my mom. But they can wait. I need to talk Evie into getting on a flight home. Although I think once she finds out Emmanuel spent the night watching her sleep, or at least I think he did, she's going to run anyway.

"Hey, I think you should get an early flight back home," I tell her.

Evie pours the coffee from the pot into a mug before turning around to face me. "Why?"

"Remember that guy from last night? The one you were flirting with?"

"Emmanuel, kinda hard to forget." She smiles.

"Yeah, well, I don't think he was kidding around about being a cartel boss, hon. When I woke up, he was holding a gun to Louie's head."

"What?" Evie shrieks, coffee spilling from her mouth.

"He wanted to wake me up and Louie wouldn't do it," I try to explain.

"You mean, the guy you just met had a gun to his head and still wouldn't wake you up?" she asks me. "That man is a keeper, Charlotte."

"Yeah, well, I did marry him. But that's not the point. Emmanuel wanted to know what happened."

"What happened when?" Evie questions.

"To you," I say gently. "He was watching you sleep. I didn't know. He left after he carried you up to the bedroom. I didn't know he came back," I tell her.

"He carried me up to bed?" She shakes her head. "Doesn't matter. What did you tell him?"

"You were talking in your sleep, Evie. He was adamant on finding out why. I didn't tell him anything other than to look into the pageant world."

Evie's eyes widen. "It doesn't matter. I'm sure he's forgotten about it by now. But you're right. I do need to get home."

"I'm sorry," I say. "I shouldn't have said anything. I know that."

"It's fine. He can dig all he wants. He's not going to find anything, because there is nothing to find. I'm glad I was here when you got married," she says.

"Me too. It's crazy, right?" I sigh.

"It is, but I think it was for the best. You seem... happy with him."

"We don't even know each other. What if it turns out he clips his toenails in bed or something just as gross? Or what if he wakes up tomorrow and decides he doesn't want to be married anymore?" I ask her.

"What if he doesn't? What if you spend the rest

of your life waking up next to him and you're both sickeningly happy? What if you get to live the dream everyone wants?" Evie counters.

"I know, but I just worry. It's all happened so fast."

"You know, there are many cultures that have arranged marriages and those work out. Is it fast? Yes, but that doesn't make it wrong," Evie says.

"How did you get so smart?"

"I don't know, but don't tell anyone because I don't need them all expecting this level of wisdom from me." Evie laughs. "Now, I'm going to shower and find a flight." She places her empty mug on the counter and walks off. Only to stop short. "He's not still around, is he?"

"Who?"

"Emmanuel?"

"I have no idea. Want me to ask Louie?"

"No, I just want to get out of here without running into him. It's creepy that he watched me sleep... and embarrassing."

"I'll make sure you don't have to see him." I don't know how, but I'll make it happen.

"Thank you for helping me," I tell Sammie as I climb into the car after dropping Evie off at the airport.

"Anytime," he says. "You're family now."

My phone vibrates in my bag. I dig around for it and quickly see I have ten missed calls. All from Louie. I frown. I didn't hear it ring. Just as I go to swipe to answer it, it cuts out.

"Boss?" Sammie says, and then Louie's voice comes over the speaker in the car.

"I can't get a hold of Charlotte and she's at the airport." He sounds... stressed.

"Ah, how do you know I'm at the airport?" I ask before Sammie adds, "Yeah, we just dropped Evie off. On our way back to the Royal now."

"You dropped Evie off?" Louie parrots.

"How do you know where I am?" I repeat, seeing as he didn't answer me the first time.

"We'll discuss it when you get back," Louie says, his voice now devoid of emotion. "No stopping. Straight here." He then cuts the call.

I look to Sammie. "Does he always just order you around like that?"

"He's in a mood. Probably because he thought you were making a run for it." He chuckles.

"How does he know where I am?"

Sammie shrugs. "No idea. You'll have to take that one up with your husband."

"You're lying, but don't worry because *I will* take it up with him," I grumble before changing the subject. "Do you have a girlfriend? Or boyfriend? Or even both?"

"Neither." He shivers, as if the mere thought of being in a relationship is the worst thing that could happen to him.

"Does Carlo?"

"No." Sammie laughs again.

"Okay then. Nice chat," I groan.

"Look, we just aren't used to this. It's always been the four of us. Mostly three, because Emmanuel was taken to Mexico and only visited on holidays. But we've always just had each other."

"And now you have me." I smile. "And Carlo has Jazzy. Do you think her mom will turn up for her? I can't believe someone would just leave their child."

"That's because you come from a good family. Good parents. We didn't all grow up like that."

Sammie turns to me. "And if she is his, then she has all of us. We're a package deal."

"I do have good parents. As much as my mother grates on my nerves, she never would have left me, and my parents worked hard to provide for us." Speaking of, I really need to call my mother. And probably my sister. I'm not ready to forgive Melanie, but I do want to make sure she's okay.

"I like you for Louie," Sammie tells me as we pull up in front of the Royal Flush Casino. "Don't hurt him."

"I won't." I couldn't imagine hurting him. "I'm just going to make a quick call before we go up."

"Okay, I'll wait outside for you."

I take a deep breath, close my eyes for a minute, and then force myself to scroll through my contacts until I find my sister's number. "Charlotte? Oh my god, I'm so glad you called. Are you okay?" she answers almost instantly.

"Am I okay?" I ask her. "You know what? I think I am... Are you?"

"I am so sorry. That should have been the first thing I said. There is no excuse for what I did. I don't know why I did it, and I really am sorry," she rushes out in one long breath.

"I don't know what to say, Melanie."

"I know."

"He's dead," I blurt, leaving out the part that I'm the reason why.

"I know. Are you okay, though? I mean, you loved him. Of course you're not okay."

"You thought I loved him and you still slept with him? How long? How long were you fucking my fiancé behind my back?" I hiss into the phone.

"I... It was only that one time, Charlotte. I swear." She starts crying.

"Stop. You don't get to cry. It was supposed to be my wedding night," I remind her.

"I know. I didn't mean to hurt you."

"We are never going to be the same. You know that, right? How am I ever going to trust you again?"

"I'll do whatever it takes. I will do anything, Charlotte. Just tell me what to do," she pleads. "Let me come to you."

"No." I shake my head, even though she can't see me, and a stray tear falls down my cheek. "I got married last night. And I don't want you anywhere near my husband. I don't trust you."

"You what? To whom? You went and got married. Your fiancé just died."

"Owen wasn't mine, though. I gotta go." I cut the call before she can ask any more questions, and a text

message from Melanie comes through almost immediately.

MELANIE:

I love you. I'm sorry.

I swipe it off my screen, pocket my phone, and
climb out of the car.

"You good?" Sammie asks me.

"Yeah." I nod. I'm not, but my issues with my
sister are just that. Mine.

Chapter Thirty-One

I panicked. When I saw Charlotte was at the airport, I thought she was leaving me. I get it. I have fucking abandonment issues. But fuck... Just the thought had me breaking out in a sweat. I can't let her go. I had no intentions of letting her go. But the thought she'd want to...

The door to the penthouse opens and Charlotte

walks in. And straight away, all of my personal shit is shoved aside. She's been crying. I stride over to her and tilt her face up. "Who made you cry?" I ask her.

Her brows draw down. "No one," she says, looking away.

"Don't lie to me, Charlotte. You've been crying."

"It was one tear. I wasn't crying and how can you even tell?"

"Because I know you. Who and why?" I press.

"It's nothing. I called my sister." She walks past me, setting her bag down on the table.

"What happened?"

"Nothing. I just wanted to check on her. I didn't know how she felt about Owen. I thought she might have been upset," Charlotte says.

"Okay. Do you want to go back to see your family? I can arrange a trip," I offer.

"Home is the last place I want to be," she says.

I reach forward and tug Charlotte against my body. "Home is where you're standing right now. This is your home, sweetheart."

"What if I don't want to live in a casino?" she says against my chest.

"Then I'll buy us a house," I tell her.

"Maybe one day, when we have kids. *If* we have

kids. I just don't think a casino is the place to raise them," she says.

"*When* we have kids, we will not have them anywhere near this cesspool," I promise her.

"How'd you know where I was today?"

"Lucky guess?" I shrug, hoping she'll drop the topic.

She shakes her head. "Try again."

"I might have put a tracking app on your phone..."

"Why?"

"I need to know where you are, Charlotte. I have... There are people that will do anything to hurt me. As soon as the world finds out you are the single most important person to me, well, you become a target," I explain cautiously. "But I'm not going to let anything happen to you."

"Okay." She sighs. "But you could have just asked me. I'll tell you where I am. I don't have anything to hide."

"I thought you were leaving me," I admit. "I didn't like it.

"I'm sorry you thought that. But I'm not going anywhere," she says. "I do need to borrow a computer, though. I need to get a resume together and find a job."

"Charlotte, you don't need a job." I finally loosen my grip on her and walk over to the kitchen.

"I actually do," she says from behind me.

I pull out two bottles of water from the fridge before handing one to Charlotte. "You own three casinos on this strip. You don't need a job."

"*You* own casinos. I don't own shit," she argues.

"We're married. What's mine is now yours. We didn't sign a prenup, sweetheart."

Her eyes widen. "Well, that was really stupid of you. Jesus, Louie, what if I was some gold-digging hussy who just wanted to take half of everything you own?"

"You're not, though." I laugh.

"But you don't know that. I could be."

"Sweetheart, you've been arguing with me for the last couple of days about needing a job. You're not a gold digger," I remind her.

"Well, it was still stupid of you to get married without paperwork. And we can just sign some now. I don't care."

"I care," I tell her. "This marriage doesn't have a timestamp, Charlotte. There's no need for a prenup because there isn't going to be a divorce." Before she can say more, I take hold of her hand and drag her over to the sofa. "I got you something today."

Reaching into my pocket, I pull out the small red box and open it.

Charlotte's eyes go round. "Oh my gosh!" she gasps.

"I shouldn't have married you without getting you a ring first," I tell her. "We can make it up, you know. Have a redo. A big fancy reception. A destination wedding. Whatever you want."

"I like the wedding we had. I don't need anything else."

I take the ring set out of the box and slide it onto Charlotte's finger.

"How did you know the size?" she asks me. "Louie, this is beautiful."

I lift a shoulder in a half-shrug. It's a single, princess-cut, diamond solitaire. Three carrots. The wedding band is rose-gold and lined with several smaller stones to complement the one in the middle.

Charlotte looks up at me. "Thank you." She smiles, then frowns. "Wait." She jumps up, and I watch as she rifles through her bag before returning with a pen. "I don't have a ring for you, but I'm going to get one," she says, taking hold of my left hand.

"I don't need a ring, Charlotte."

"I want you to have one. How else will all the women know you're spoken for?" she asks me.

"Because I'll tell them." I chuckle.

"Well, until I get to a store, this will do." She proceeds to draw two lines around my ring finger before adding letters to the middle.

"CG?" I ask her.

"Charlotte Giuliani. Now everyone will know you're mine." She smiles.

Leaning forward, I press my lips against hers. "Everyone will know I'm yours because I'm going to scream it from the rooftops," I tell her.

I open the door and step aside so Paulie can enter. "Thanks for coming."

"No problem. What do you need?" he asks me.

"It won't take long. Come on through." I lead Paulie to the dining table and sit down. "I want you to ink over this." I hold out my left hand.

Paulie coughs. "You're serious?"

"Deadly." I glare at him.

"O... kay then." He starts pulling his equipment out of his bag. "You get hitched or something?"

"I did. Last night."

"Congratulations," he says. "Gotta say, I'm a little surprised. I didn't know you were seeing anyone."

"It was fast." I smile.

Just as Paulie is cleaning me off and packing up again, Charlotte comes out. She just showered and got changed. I want to take her on a proper date. She's wearing a red dress that reaches her knees, but it's fucking tight, hugging all of her curves and leaving absolutely nothing to the imagination. Her hair hangs in loose waves down her back.

Fuck, she's beautiful. And she's all mine.

"Paulie, this is Charlotte, my wife," I introduce her. "Paulie is my artist."

"Your artist, as in tattoo artist?" she asks. "What are you getting done?"

"Already done." I hold up my hand, showing her my finger.

"You didn't." She smiles huge as she takes hold of my hand to get a closer look.

"I did. It's never coming off," I tell her.

"Can you do mine?" Charlotte looks to Paulie. "The same?"

"Absolutely fucking not," I growl.

"Why not?" Charlotte glares at me.

Great, this is going to be another fight.

kylie Kent

"Because you don't need your body marred by anything," I tell her. "Also, I'm not having another man touch you."

"It's a finger, and it's not marring. It's... symbolic. If you don't want Paulie to do it, then you can do it yourself."

"I'm not hurting you." I shake my head, dismissing the idea.

"It won't hurt," she tells me.

"Yeah? How many tattoos you got, sweetheart?" I ask her, knowing damn well she has none. I've inspected every inch of her body. It's a blank canvas.

"None, but I'm also not a wimp. I can handle whatever it feels like." She crosses her arms over her chest.

I reach out a hand to Paulie, and he takes it. "Thanks." Poor guy looks like he'd rather be anywhere else right now.

"It was nice meeting you, Mrs. Giuliani." He nods and then makes a beeline for the door.

"That is not fair, Louie," Charlotte pouts.

"Life isn't fair, sweetheart," I tell her.

"Don't *sweetheart* me. Besides, this is Vegas. I'll just drop into any old shop and get it done."

I pull my phone from my pocket and message Paulie before he has time to even leave the building.

324

ME:

> Make sure every shop on the strip
> knows not to touch her.

PAULIE:

> On it.

"Sure, you do that. You ready to go?" I turn to Charlotte. "You look absolutely stunning by the way. I should have already said that."

"Thank you. Where are we going?" she asks.

"I have reservations for dinner, and then whatever else you want to do."

"Can we gamble? After dinner? I just realized I haven't so much as put a dollar into a slot machine since I got here. Seems like a crime."

"That's not a crime. That's just smart. The house always wins," I tell her. "But since it's our house, we can gamble as much as you want."

I watch Charlotte from across the table. She's fidgeting. "What's wrong?" I ask her.

"People are staring," she whispers.

"That's because you're beautiful and they're

wondering how I managed to score you."

"No, they're not." She laughs.

"How do you know?" I lift a challenging brow and then look around the restaurant. Watching how everyone quickly averts their eyes.

"They're looking at you," Charlotte says.

"Do you want to leave?" I should have known I couldn't just come out for a meal like a normal fucking person.

"No, I want to eat. I just need to get used to ignoring people," she tells me. "It's hard, because I've spent my whole life having to care what people think, and I'm scared of making a bad impression. I don't want to embarrass you."

"Charlotte, you could never embarrass me." I stand, pick up my glass of champagne, and tap a fork against the side.

"What are you doing?" Charlotte gasps.

"Ladies and gentleman, I want you all to be the first to know I was lucky enough to have this woman right here marry me last night. I'm officially off the market, and so is she," I announce to the crowd of onlookers. Claps and cheers erupt around us as I lean forward and press a kiss to Charlotte's lips. "I really am the luckiest motherfucker alive," I tell her before sitting back down. "Now they'll have something to really talk about."

"Thank you." Charlotte smiles at me. "I don't know how, but you always know the right thing to say."

"You should hear my inside thoughts, then." I quirk a brow with a different kind of challenge this time.

"What are your inside thoughts right now?" she asks me.

"How I want to swipe everything off this table and replace it with your body. How I want to spread your legs wide open and feast on nothing but you all night long." I keep my voice low.

Charlotte's face reddens. "Yeah, ah... let's not say that out loud." She smirks before adding, "Well, at least not in public."

Chapter Thirty-Two

Charlotte

Louie hands me a stack of chips. Chips that say one thousand on them. "This is too much. I thought we were just going to drop a dollar or two into a slot machine," I tell him.

"If we're going to gamble, Charlotte, we're doing it properly," he says, holding a case full of chips in one hand. His other hand lands on my lower back.

"Besides, you're my good luck charm. I have a feeling I'm going to win tonight."

"Ah, Louie, you're the house, remember? You win every night," I whisper.

"Even more so now that I have you in my bed."

We end up in front of a roulette table. "I don't actually know how to do any of this," I admit. Which is why a slot machine would have been the better choice. There isn't much to them.

"It's easy. Place a chip on any number or you can do more than one. You can also bet on red or black by placing a chip here or here." Louie points to various spots on the table. "Or you can bet on odd or even, or high and low numbers. Take your pick," he says.

"I can do two numbers?" I ask him.

"You can." Louie nods.

I look through the chips in my hand. "Do you have anything lower? This is a lot of money to lose."

"Sweetheart, even if we lose, it goes back into the casino, which we own," he reminds me.

"Right." Okay, so I'm not really gambling with thousands of dollars here. *I can do this.* I put a thousand-dollar chip on four and then another on sixteen.

"My lucky numbers," Louie says.

"Hey, they're mine. Get your own." I laugh. It's yesterday's date, the day we got married.

"They can be ours." He wraps an arm around my waist.

I don't miss the way women are openly gaping at us, most sending daggers my way. Louie either doesn't notice or pretends not to.

"Watch." He nods at the dealer, who spins the wheel. The little ball goes around and around until it slowly stops on the number four.

"Did we win?" I ask.

"You won." He chuckles in my ear, his chest pressing against my back.

I jump up and spin around with excitement before my arms wrap around his neck. "I told you they were lucky numbers."

"The luckiest," he agrees.

I push up on my tiptoes and press my lips against his. I can never get enough of kissing him. I still think I'm locked in some kind of dream and this isn't really my life right now.

"Come on, we've got more games to learn," Louie tells me.

We end up at a card table. Louie pulls out a chair for me while he stands at my back. "What is this game?" I ask him.

"Black Jack. It's easy." He places another pile of chips in front of me.

The dealer hands out two cards to everyone. I pick up mine. I know you have to make twenty-one to win, or get as close to it as you can. I just got dealt a queen of hearts and an ace of spades.

"Queen of hearts, that's you," Louie whispers in my ear. "You're my queen of hearts. And you've already won the game."

"Really? I won again?" I shriek.

The other players at the table groan and glare at me. That is until Louie turns to them. "Problem?" he asks.

"No, sir." All three men shake their heads.

"I didn't fucking think so," Louie says. He lifts me from the chair, holding me upright until I'm stable on my feet. "Let's go find a poker game. You really are my lucky charm." He then swipes up my winning hand before turning to the dealer. "Get a new deck. I'm keeping these."

The cards are black and gold with the royal flush symbol on the back. I don't know who does Louie's marketing, but they're good. Because even the playing cards in this place look high end.

"What's next?" I ask. "Also, just in case I forget to tell you later, I had a really good time tonight. You're not too shabby at this dating thing."

"I'll have to up my game if *not too shabby* is all

I'm rated." He laughs. "I'm going to wine and dine the fuck out of you, Mrs. Giuliani."

I spin around and walk backwards so I'm looking directly at him. "I can't wait to be wined and dined by you." I smile, my feet coming to a stop when Louie wraps an arm around my waist again.

"I love you," he says. His lips descend towards mine. And just before they reach, a glint of something behind him catches my eye.

No, not something. A gun. Pointed right at Louie's back. I push him to the side. Which must *catch* him off guard, because somehow I end up in front of him as he stumbles out of the way. And then a sharp burning pain tears through my right shoulder.

Screaming. There's so much screaming. I stumble back. Into a body.

"Fuck, Charlotte!" Louie shouts. His arms wrap around me, and I lean against him as we both fall to the casino floor.

No. He wasn't hit. He couldn't have been.

I pushed him out of the way. I know I did. But Louie is still screaming, and chaos is erupting everywhere. I see guns, so many guns. Followed by loud bangs, which send a high-pitched ringing through my ears.

I look up at Louie. "I love you," I tell him, my voice barely above a whisper.

"Don't..." Louie growls. "I need a fucking ambulance now!" He calls out over the deafening noise, his hand pressing against my shoulder.

It hurts. I close my eyes. I can feel sleep pulling me under. If I sleep, maybe it won't hurt so bad.

"Charlotte, don't you dare leave me! Stay with me, sweetheart, please." Louie's voice has my lashes fluttering open. "That's it. Look at me. You said you wouldn't leave me. Why would you do that? Why would you jump in front of a fucking bullet?"

"Because I didn't want it to hit you," I tell him.

"Where the fuck is the ambulance?" Louie yells out again.

"I'm just gonna sleep for a little bit."

"No. Don't!" This time, Louie sounds like he's underwater. Or maybe I am. I like being underwater. It's calming here.

Chapter Thirty-Three

"How the fuck did someone get a gun into my casino?" My voice echoes off the walls of the hospital hallway. There's no one here, bar the doctors and nurses surrounding Charlotte.

My wife. One fucking day with my last name attached, and I've already failed her. It's my job to keep her safe, and she was shot in my own fucking house.

"He was a dealer," Carlo says, looking over a shoulder to where Jazzy is sitting on one of the shitty plastic chairs. He put a pair of noise canceling headphones on the kid and gave her an iPad. Judging by the way she doesn't budge at my outburst, I'd say she can't hear shit right now.

"A dealer." I shake my head. "Everyone's been vetted." *How could this happen? With one of my own staff?*

"He was related to that Greggory fuck. Cousins, from what I hear."

"Who the fuck is Greggory?" I grunt.

"The kid we offed last week, the one Justin squealed to about the drop spot," Sammie says.

I run my hands through my hair. "Where the fuck is Emmanuel?" I haven't seen or heard from him since yesterday.

"No idea." Carlo shrugs. "He's gone off the grid."

"Fucking hell. We're supposed to be collecting a shipment in three hours." I can't leave this hospital. I can't leave her. What if she wakes up and I'm not fucking here?

"I got it," Sammie tells me.

"You can't go without backup," I remind him.

"Especially when we don't know if this fucking asshole was working alone. What else do we know about Greggory?"

"Nothing. He had no links to any known family. He was just a street thug."

"We're missing something. Find it," I hiss. "And take the kid home. She shouldn't be stuck here."

I sigh, looking towards the glass that separates us from my wife's lifeless body. Sprawled out on the hospital bed. The doctors assured me she'd pull through. They got the bullet out, and they said it missed anything vital. Which means she should be waking the fuck up.

"I'll come with you to the drop," I tell Sammie. I can't let him go alone. "I want this whole fucking hospital surrounded. I want ten men in this hallway, and I want them all warned that if anything happens to her, it's their lives they'll pay with."

The doors open and Emmanuel walks in. "She okay?"

"Where the fuck have you been?" I grunt.

Was it him? Did he have something to do with that kid pulling the trigger? A bullet that was supposed to be aimed for me and not my wife.

"I went to track down a contact. I heard what happened and came back," he says.

The doors push open again and Charlotte's friend comes running down the hall. The same one who was supposed to be on a flight out of here. "Where is she?" Evie screams. "What the hell did you do?" Her fists slam against my chest the moment she reaches me.

Emmanuel grabs her around the waist and pulls her back. "Whoa, it wasn't him," he tells her.

"If it weren't *for him*, nothing would have happened to her. Where is..." Evie stops short when she spots Charlotte through the window. "No!"

"She's going to be okay," I tell her. "She's going to wake up."

Evie glares at me, shakes out of Emmanuel's hold, and walks into the hospital room.

"Tracking down a contact or stalking an unsuspecting woman?" Sammie muses.

"Shut the fuck up," Emmanuel hisses at him.

"We've got a shipment coming in. I need to go and get it," I tell Emmanuel. "You gonna stick around?"

"I'll go. You stay," he says. "I know what you think. But it wasn't fucking me, Louie. You really need to get over your hangups. I'm not out to fucking shoot you in the back. We both know I'd do it while you were looking right at me."

"My wife is lying unconscious in a fucking hospital bed. Forgive me for not trusting you!" I yell at him.

"Remember, that's your wife's best friend. You can't kill her." He smirks. "I'll be back. Let's go, Sammie."

"You know it's pretty fucked up, you collecting your own product," Sammie replies.

"You know what else is fucked up? The sound of your fucking voice," Emmanuel throws back at him as they walk out.

"Uncle Louie, when my mama was in the hospital, I used to play music for her. It would always make her happy. Maybe you can play music for Charlotte." Jazzy's little voice has me looking down.

"Your mama was in the hospital?" I ask, and the little girl nods her head. Carlo hasn't been able to get anything out of the kid about her mother. It's fucking weird. Most kids would at least slip and say a name or something. "Well, thanks for the tip. I'll have to try it."

"I'm going to take her home." Carlo looks to me. "You gonna be good here?"

"Yep, dig into the asshole. I want to know if he was working alone or not," I tell him.

"On it," he says, scooping Jazzy up and walking out.

I push into the room and sit next to Charlotte. I pull out my phone. I want to play her something and I have no fucking idea what music she likes. "Fuck!"

My fist clenches. She's my wife. I should know what kind of fucking music she likes. Why didn't I ask her more questions?

"Are you okay?" Evie says.

"My wife was shot. So, no, I'm not fucking okay," I grunt at her.

"What happened?"

"She jumped in front of a bullet that was meant for me." *It was supposed to be me.*

"She loves you." Evie nods. "You would have done the same thing... if you were the one who saw it coming. Right?"

"Of course I would have." My hands run through my hair. "I don't know what music she likes. I need to play her music and I don't know what kind she likes."

"Charlotte, if you don't wake up, I'm going to tell him you love Tay-Tay and that's all you're going to hear until you wake up," Evie says to Charlotte, who doesn't fucking budge. Evie looks at me again. "Why isn't she waking up?"

"They said she will, in her own time."

"Well, that time could be now." Evie nods, like it's a done deal. Even though we both know it's not. "She likes country. Just put on any country mix and she will love it."

Fucking country. Great. I hate country. But I'll listen to it until my ears bleed if it means she'll wake up.

"You think she can hear us?" I ask Evie.

She shakes her head. "I don't know..."

Four hours later, Evie steps out of the room to get coffee. I can't leave. My hand grips Charlotte's tighter. I put her wedding rings back on after they brought her out of surgery. I wasn't having all these doctors and nurses standing around, thinking she's not married. I should have let Paulie put that tattoo on her. Maybe I'll do it myself when she wakes up.

Charlottes fingers move. My head snaps up and my eyes connect with hers. "You're awake." I sigh out a breath of relief. "Thank fuck. I was so fucking scared," I tell her, leaning down to press my lips to the center of her forehead. "I'm so sorry."

"Am I still dreaming?" Charlotte asks, her face full of confusion.

"No, sweetheart. You're not dreaming unless I am."

"I had a dream. I married someone. *You*. But that's not real. Men like you don't fall for girls like me, so I'm definitely still dreaming." She smiles at me.

"I didn't just fall for you, Mrs. Giuliani. I jumped over that cliff without a rope. There's no undoing it. I love you."

"I love you," she says. "Are you okay? You weren't hurt, were you?"

"I've aged at least fifty years from the worry. Don't ever do that again. You are not allowed to risk yourself for anyone," I tell her.

"Mmm, you're not my dad. You can't tell me what to do," she says. "I need..."

"What? What do you need?" *Shit!* I press the call button for the nurses or doctors or whoever. They should know she's awake.

"Water," Charlotte rasps out, and I immediately reach for a plastic cup. I fill it with some ice water from the pitcher and drop a straw inside before I hold the whole thing up to her mouth.

"Don't move," I tell her.

Charlotte sips at the straw until the room is rushed by a crowd of doctors and nurses. And I am forced to step aside while they all fuss over her.

Evie comes back in shortly after. "Oh my god, you're awake. Why didn't you tell me she woke up?" She glares at me. I'm guessing I'm not making the woman's Christmas card list anytime soon. I also don't give a shit. Which is why I don't answer her.

"What are you doing here? You went home," Charlotte asks Evie.

"I... ah... ran into a little obstacle. We'll talk about it later. I'm just so glad you're awake. You scared the crap out of me. Don't do that again," Evie tells her.

The doctor leaves after giving Charlotte strict orders not to move from the bed. She looks to me as soon as the door clicks closed again. "What happened? To the guy?"

"Security got him seconds after he fired the shot," I tell her.

"Why was he trying to shoot you, though?"

"I don't know. We're looking into it."

"Okay. But you're going to be safe, right? No one

is actively trying to kill you?" Charlotte stares at me pleadingly.

"I'm not going anywhere," I assure her.

Charlotte nods before turning to Evie. "Now, you. Why are you back?"

"Shit, it's my mom. I gotta take this." Evie waves at her phone, which isn't even ringing, and runs out the door.

"Emmanuel brought her here," I explain.

"Louie?"

"Yeah?"

"I want to go home," Charlotte says.

"I'm going to take you home, as soon as the doctor says I can," I promise her.

"Will you stay with me?" she asks.

"I'm not going anywhere."

"Thank you." She smiles and yawns.

"Thank *you*. You literally saved my life today, sweetheart, but don't do it again."

"It's what wives do," she says, her eyes fluttering closed. "I like being your wife."

la Docena

Chapter Thirty-Four

Q♡ Charlotte

It's been a week since I was shot, and I finally get to go home. I kept asking the staff when I was going to be released, but I think Louie had warned the doctor to keep me in that damn hospital for as long as possible. He's not overly happy over the fact I've been discharged.

The car stops out front of the Royal Flush. I

know I was itching to come home, but having to walk through the casino again.... Yeah, I'm not so sure about that. A light sheen of sweat covers my forehead and my heart picks up speed at the thought.

"Louie, I..." I look at him. I don't know what to say.

"I've got you. You are safe here, Charlotte. I promise," he says.

"But are *you*?" I ask him.

"Yes."

"I don't know if I can go in there," I admit.

"We'll use the staff entrance. You don't have to go onto the casino floor," he says. "Come on." He opens the door, jumps down from the SUV, and then reaches in and picks me up.

"What are you doing? Put me down. I can walk," I tell him.

"No," he says, walking inside the casino before making a quick left.

"What do you mean *no*? I can walk, Louie. Put me down," I repeat.

"And I can carry you. *I want to*," he says.

I don't realize the death grip I have on him until we enter his penthouse and he sets me down on the bed. He has to pry my hands from his shirt so he can stand. Though he does appear reluctant to do it.

"Don't move," Louie instructs before turning and walking out of the room.

I get up and follow him. Pain goes straight through to my shoulder, but I push through it. I'm not sitting around in bed for another week.

"What are you doing? You need to be in bed," Louie says.

"No, I really don't. I'm going to sit on the sofa," I tell him, making my way through to the living room.

He brings me a bottle of water and sits next to me. "Are you in pain? Do you need anything?"

I shake my head. "I don't need anything. Just you."

True to his word, Louie didn't leave my side for the entirety of the week I spent at the hospital. There were times he'd walk outside the room to talk to Sammie or Carlo, but he'd always stand where he could see me. Where I could see *him*.

"I really do appreciate you staying with me. I know you have a lot of work to do," I tell him after a moment of silence.

"I wouldn't be anywhere else, Charlotte. You're my wife. That makes you my number one priority. If you need me, then I'm going to be there. Always," Louie says.

"You don't have to stay now if there are things you need to do. I'll be okay."

"I'm not leaving you alone."

"Evie and Rachel are here," I remind him.

"Evie and Rachel aren't me," he replies. "I don't think I'm ready to leave you just yet."

"Then don't." I don't care how long he stays glued to my side. I like it. At least I know he's safe, and no one is trying to kill him.

The few times I've asked Louie about the guy, about what happens next, he's shut me down with vague answers. I know he doesn't want me to worry, but I don't know how I can let him walk out that door and not worry. I was engaged to a police officer and I never once worried about Owen not coming home. I always knew it was a possibility. It didn't faze me. But the thought of Louie walking out the door and not coming back has my heart increasing and my palms sweaty.

Sammie and Carlo pop in a few minutes later. "Boss, a word," Sammie says, nodding his head towards the hall that leads to Louie's home office.

"I'll be right back." Louie stands before placing a kiss to the middle of my forehead.

Carlo comes and sits next to me. He looks nervous. *What the hell is going on?*

"I have a question. It's a girl thing," he says.

"Pretty sure you're past that talk." I laugh. "What's up?"

"Not that type of question. It's Jazzy. She keeps asking me to braid her hair. I don't know how to fucking braid hair and no matter how many YouTube videos I watch, I can't get it right," he says.

"Okay, first of all, braids are not just a girl thing. Second, it's easy. I'll teach you." I run my fingers through to the end of my hair. Pulling it over my shoulder before I separate the strands. "You need to start with three sections and just cross them over each other like this." I demonstrate a few pleats before handing my hair to him. "Here, you keep going."

Carlo looks behind us and then back at me. "If I die, I've made you and Louie Jazzy's guardians," he tells me, taking hold of the strands.

"You're not dying." I roll my eyes.

"I might... in a few minutes." He laughs, his fingers fumbling as he attempts to braid my hair. He is really bad. I didn't think braiding hair was that difficult.

"Is there a reason you're touching my wife's hair, or are you just looking to lose your fucking hands?" Louie growls—yes, growls—as he storms towards us.

"Relax. I was teaching him how to braid. For Jazzy. But it might be a lost cause." I look from my husband, back to Carlo. "Just bring her over and I'll do it for her."

"Get a fucking doll and practice. Don't touch my wife," Louie grunts. He then turns to face me, and his whole demeanor softens. "Sweetheart, I have to go downstairs and deal with something real quick. Will you be okay here?"

I want to say no. I want to tell him not to leave me. But he has to work. He's a busy man, and I can't be needy. "I'll be fine. Evie and Rachel are coming over."

They're both staying in the suite next door. Rachel flew out here as soon as she heard what happened to me. I thought Louie was bad at hovering. But having an actual doctor for a best friend? Yeah, she's put that man to shame.

I made the girls promise not to tell anyone about my injury. The last thing I need is my parents flying out here because I was shot. Besides, I'm fine. I don't need to worry them.

"Carlo, go get the girls and tell them they need to come now," Louie says. "At least one of them is a doctor." He says *this* under his breath, as if he's trying to assure himself he can leave me.

"I'll be fine. Go work. Do whatever you have to do." I never thought I'd say it, but I miss working. I wonder if I can help out around the casino. But then the thought of actually going downstairs sends panic through me.

I count to five in my head and take deep breaths as casually as I can. I don't want Louie to think I'm panicking. I'm not. It's just a little blip in my system. I'm going to be fine.

As soon as Carlo returns with the girls, Louie leaves. We sit on the sofa together, and I let Evie flick through Netflix, trying to decide on something to watch. Until a loud bang has me jumping and screaming. I curl into a ball, my arms wrapping around my legs.

"Sorry, it was just my phone," Rachel says. "Charlotte, you're safe. It's okay." Her hands run up and down my back.

"I'm okay," I breathe out. I don't like sudden noises so much. I can still hear the gunshots when I close my eyes. I look to the door. I need Louie. "Do you think he's okay?"

"He's fine," Evie tells me. "That man is scarier than the devil himself."

"Says the one hanging around a cartel boss." I scowl at her. "Speaking of, where is your shadow today?"

"He went back to Mexico," she says. "And he's not my anything."

"Sure he's not." I look to the door before swiping up my phone. "I need to know."

"You're going to call him? Charlotte, he just left ten minutes ago," Evie reminds me.

"I know. You're right. He's fine." I set my phone back down on the table. *He is fine. He has to be.*

I don't know how much time passes, but I'm shaking. Literally, my hands are shaking. My heart is pounding, and all I can think about is Louie on the floor surrounded by blood. I can't get the picture out of my head. No matter how much I try. Tears fall down my cheeks, and I swipe them away.

"Shit. Charlotte, babe, what's wrong?" Rachel asks, jumping up and dropping down so that she's now kneeling in front of me.

"I can't... I don't..." I can't seem to find the words. "Louie..."

"I'll get him." Evie snatches up my phone and

holds it to my face to unlock the screen. I don't hear what she says. I don't hear what either of my friends are telling me.

"Fucking hell, what the fuck happened?" That's the one thing I do hear, though. Louie's voice. I turn my head to see him charging towards me.

"She's having a panic attack," Rachel says.

"Why?" Louie asks her. His arms slide underneath me and he picks me up. I don't hear anything else as he carries me into the bedroom. He sits on the bed and holds me against his chest. "It's okay. Just breathe, Charlotte. I've got you. You're okay. I love you."

He continues to whisper soft words into my ear while stroking his fingers through my hair. My own fingers cling to the lapels of his jacket. "I'm sorry," I manage to say.

"It's okay. You don't have to be sorry," he tells me.

"I couldn't stop thinking about you. I could see it, Louie. I could see you on the floor, covered in blood," I explain. "And I wasn't there to move you out of the way."

"I'm right here, Charlotte. I'm fine. *We* are fine," he says, placing a soft kiss to the top of my head.

"I'm sorry," I repeat. I don't want to be this

person, the one who can't handle being away from her husband. I don't want to be consumed by fear.

"We found him," Louie says.

"What? You found who?" I ask him.

"Sammie found the guy who organized the hit," he clarifies. "It was a rival family, and they've been dealt with."

"What do you mean a rival family?"

"Another family working the strip. They were trying to one-up me. They failed, and now they're paying the price. The guy who orchestrated it... He's gone. He's not going to be a problem anymore."

"How do you know that family won't try again?"

"Because we came to an agreement. There's going to be a wedding," Louie tells me. "Don't worry about it. Like I said, it's dealt with. You don't have to worry about me, Charlotte. I promise nothing is ever going to take me away from you."

I cling tighter to him as another tear streams down my cheek. "I love you more than I thought was humanly possible."

"I love you too, sweetheart. You have no idea how much..."

Chapter Thirty-Five

An Hour Earlier

Deep down, I know Charlotte wasn't okay with me leaving her. She's not alone, though. She has her friends with her. And if I didn't have to sort out the shitshow that is our fucking world, I wouldn't have left.

Sammie and Carlo found the fucker who arranged that hit on me. It was a member of the Marciano family. They're Italian mafia, and they're trying to gain a foothold here on the strip. My fucking strip.

Because their Don is someone I respect, I've agreed to have a sit down with him. That doesn't mean I'm not going to hang the fucker responsible for putting that bullet in my wife. Slaughter him like the pig he is. By his own hand or not, he's the reason Charlotte was put in danger. The reason she was shot, instead of me. Death is the kindest thing I can do for him.

Joey Marciano sits across from me. I meet his glare with one of my own. "Make this quick. You and I both know I'm not going to let him live. My wife was shot because some asshole thought making a move on my casino was a smart thing to do. So, what-ever you have to tell yourself in order to come to terms with one of your men being taken out by me, I suggest you do it."

"I'm not here to start a war with you, Giuliani," Joey says.

"Then why are you here?"

"I have a gift. For you." The old bastard smiles. "A show of good will." He waves a hand, and his underboss opens the door. A man is tossed inside, hitting the floor with an audible *thud* before scrambling to his knees. "The guy you're looking for." Joey nods in the fucker's direction.

"What's the catch?" I ask, not moving from my seat. No matter how much I want to get my hands on that fucker. I haven't gotten to where I am today by acting on emotion. I'm not going to start now. I have so much more to fucking live for.

"What? Boss, no, don't do this! I didn't do anything! I swear!" The fucker screams while trying to get to his feet. A hard task when your ankles and wrists are still bound.

"I want to make a deal. One that will benefit both of our organizations," Joey says. "One where this..." He waves a hand towards his guy. "...is forgiven, forgotten."

"My wife was shot. That's not something I'll ever forget. Or forgive," I tell Joey.

"Understandable." He nods his head.

"That said, it would be rude of me to not at least hear you out." I lean back in my seat. "What kind of deal we talking?"

"A merger. Of families," Joey says. "I have a daughter, Antonia. Twenty-one, marrying age."

I blink. This fucker cannot be for real. He wants

to marry off his daughter? To whom? We don't fucking work like that.

"We're not in the business of arranged marriages," I remind him.

"It will bring peace to our two organizations, Louie. Think about it," he says. "Antonia will be married regardless. It will either be to one of your men or someone from another family." Joey sits back, mimicking my position as one leg crosses over the other.

I get the hidden message. It's us or them. One of the other crime families in Vegas. As far as I'm concerned, he can go and join *them*. I don't give a shit. All I want is that asshole squirming on the floor.

"I'll do it." Carlo steps up from behind me.

I turn to look at him. "Excuse me?" I blink.

"I'll do it. I'll marry her. For the family," he says. "It's a good idea."

"You want to enter into an arranged marriage?" I ask him.

"Sure." He lifts a shoulder.

"Fine." I turn back to Joey. I will deal with Carlo later. I don't know why the fuck someone so insistent on never getting married all of a sudden wants to enter into an arrangement with someone he doesn't even fucking know. "Let's make a deal." I hold out a hand.

The older man returns the gesture with a smile. "This is going to be a very beneficial relationship between our families," Joey says.

I nod my head. Waiting for Marciano and his underboss to leave the room before collecting my gift.

"Let's get him to the basement," I tell Sammie. I stand to button my jacket, and just as I reach for my phone, Charlotte's name flashes across the screen. I swipe to answer the call and immediately press the device to my ear. "Sweetheart? You okay?"

"It's Evie. You have to come back, Louie. Now!"

"What happened?" I ask, already walking towards the door.

"She's asking for you. Just get back," Evie says, then cuts the call.

"Fuck!" I draw my gun from behind my back. "I wanted to make this hurt a lot fucking more but I'm needed elsewhere," I tell the asshole on the floor before putting one bullet in his head and then two more into his chest.

I run to the elevators, my mind going through all the worst-case scenarios. I knew I shouldn't have fucking left her.

When I get to the apartment, I find Charlotte on the sofa. She's covered in sweat, and tears stain her cheeks. I was gone for one hour. One fucking hour.

I take her into my arms, carry her into our room, and shut the door. She doesn't need anyone else. All she needs is me. I'm not leaving her again. I don't care if I have to spend the rest of our lives by her side 24/7. I will find a way to make it work, because I never want to see her like this again.

After getting her to calm down, I tell her that I love her and lay her next to me on the bed. "I'm not going anywhere, sweetheart."

She's grabbing on to my suit like she's afraid I might disappear. "I'm sorry." Charlotte shakes out her hands as she lets go of my jacket.

"I'm going to stand up and take off my clothes. Then I'm going to carry you into the bathroom and we're going to shower together," I explain, keeping my voice cool and even.

"Can we have a bath? Or go to the pool?" she asks me.

"You can't swim just yet. But we can fill up the tub and do our best to keep your shoulder from getting too wet," I tell her as I shrug out of my jacket. I remove my shirt next and then pick her up.

"Louie, who's getting married?" Charlotte asks after we've settled into the tub.

"Carlo," I say. "He volunteered to marry the daughter of the other family."

"Why would he do that?"

"I have no idea. Maybe he saw how great our marriage is working out for us and wants what we have," I suggest.

"Maybe he thinks he needs a woman around for Jazzy," Charlotte counters.

That makes sense, but I still don't think that's the reason. He seemed... eager to be the one marrying that girl. He doesn't even know what she looks like. At least I don't think he does. For all I know, their paths could have crossed at some point. Vegas isn't as big of a city as some might think.

Epilogue

Ten years later

Sometimes I stare at my husband in awe—okay, a lot of the times I stare at him in awe. I often pinch my arm just to make sure I'm not dreaming. Because even after ten years of being with Louie, I feel like I've won the damn lottery.

Everyone thought we were crazy, getting married after only knowing each other for a little more than a weekend. *I* thought I was crazy. But now, when I look back, I realize that I knew it the moment I first saw him. I knew it when he took me up to the rooftop pool and watched me swim.

I loved this man from the moment I saw him. At the time, I was confused. I was supposed to be heart-broken after finding my fiancé in bed with my sister. Instead, it was the best thing to ever happen to me.

I turn and watch Melanie push my daughter on the swing. It took years before I was ready to let my sister fully back into my life. We don't have the same relationship we once had, or the trust, but she is my sister and I *trust* my husband. Plus, Melanie is a great aunt to my kids.

Yes, *kids*, plural. Louie and I have three. Our oldest son is nine. We got pregnant not long after we were married. Alfie is a carbon copy of his father. Then we have Hudson, our middle child, who is everything you'd expect from a middle child. He's seven. While Frankie, our youngest and only girl, is five. She's smart, strong, and fiercely independent. Unless she's around her father, and then she becomes a little princess who lets him do everything for her.

I have the life I always dreamed of. A family that is full of love, happiness, and endless adventures. My heart bursts with joy as I watch my children run around our yard, playing with their cousins.

"Sweetheart, you doing okay?" Louie sits beside me on the sun lounger. We're grilling today. We have everyone here. Carlo and his wife and kids. Sammie and his wife. And my sister, who is determined to remain unmarried forever. Rachel and Evie are here with their families as well.

"I don't know how you managed to get everyone in one place at the same time." I smile at my husband. "But I love that you did."

"It was easy. I threatened to kill them all if they didn't show up." He smirks.

Life with Louie is never boring. Do I still worry every time he leaves the house? Yes. But I've learned to deal with that worry. Because I wouldn't want to live without him.

He keeps me out of his business as much as possible. Although I don't tend to ask too many questions anymore either. I know what he does. I don't try to rationalize the good and bad in my head. I love this man. More than that, I am loved *by him* in a way I've never been loved before.

"You complete me," I say.

"I love you." Louie leans over and presses his lips to mine.

"Gross." Hudson sprays us with a water gun. "You two need to cool down." He laughs before running off.

"That kid has good aim." Louie smiles proudly.

"*That kid* is going to get into more trouble than the other two combined." I laugh.

"Yeah, probably. But we will be there to bail him out." Louie picks up my hand.

"We should do this more often. Get everyone together," I say. "It's nice having everyone here."

"It is," Louie agrees.

"Daddy, Daddy, catch me." Frankie comes barreling towards us before jumping right into Louie's arms. "You did it!" she yells out.

"I will always catch you, princess," Louie tells her.

"I know," Frankie says as if there is no other possibility.

"Okay, come on, you. We gotta get dessert out of the kitchen. You can help with the cookies," I tell Frankie, plucking her from Louie's arms.

"I made good cookies, Daddy. You'll see," Frankie says before running into the house.

I smile after her, my eyes flicking towards Louie again. "Be right back."

Louie

Ten years of pure bliss. I never knew life could be like this. I didn't know that you could love someone and they'd actually love you back with everything they had. I found Charlotte when I wasn't looking for her. She is my gift from God, a gift I'm sure I wasn't supposed to get.

She is mine, though. And nothing will ever change that.

She tells me all the time that I complete her. She has it wrong, though. She saved me from a world of nothing but darkness. She gave me light, something to come home to every night. And she gave me a family.

Our three kids are amazing. I know every parent thinks their kids are the best or whatever. But ours really are. They're half of Charlotte, and she's the best person I know. So it only makes sense that our kids came out just as amazing as she is.

Charlotte has been talking about hosting a barbecue for months now. I finally made it happen. I sent the jets to pick up everyone she loves. Personally, I couldn't give a fuck if it was just us and our kids forever. I don't need anyone else. But she loves these fuckers.

"Boss, you see the headlines?" Sammie asks while passing me his phone.

"*Suspected Underworld Crime Leader, Louie Giuliani, Set to Open Sixth Casino on the Las Vegas Strip,*" I read it aloud.

I told Charlotte I was going to buy a casino for each of our kids. I want them to have something that's just theirs. The latest one is Frankie's, and when she turns twenty-five, it'll be signed over to her completely.

"You guys aren't talking about work, are you?" Charlotte appears at my side again.

"At a family event? I wouldn't dream of it." I wrap my arm around her.

"And that's my cue." Sammie gets up and walks over to his own wife as Charlotte's hands clasp behind my neck.

"You're a terrible liar. It's a good thing you're the house, because you'd lose all your money at the poker table."

"I happen to be great at poker." I grin. "I just can't lie to you."

"Good. 'Cause we're playing later tonight. If you

beat me, we'll try for that fourth kid you want," she says.

"And if you win?" I ask her.

"Then we'll try for that fourth kid *I* want." She smiles.

We'd discussed having another one a while back. Charlotte wanted to wait until Frankie really got out of that baby stage, though. That was a few years ago, and then I guess shit just got busy. It still is. But I'm not going to tell her that. If my wife wants another child, then she's going to get another child.

"I can't wait to impregnate you again," I tell her.

"That's because you have a thing for pregnant women, weirdo."

"No, I have a thing for you, Mrs. Giuliani. Because you're *my wife*." My hand wraps around the back of Charlotte's neck, and I pull her mouth onto mine. My tongue dives in, deepening the kiss.

I will never *not* want to kiss this woman. I can't get enough of her, even after ten years.

Also by kylie Kent

The Merge Series

Merged With Him (Zac and Alyssa's Story)

Fused With Him (Bray and Reilly's Story)

Entwined With Him (Dean and Ella's Story)

2nd Generation Merge Series

Ignited by Him (Ash and Breanna's Story)

An Entangled Christmas: A Merge Series Christmas Novel (Alex and Lily's Story)

Chased By him (Chase & Hope's Story)

Tethered To Him (Noah & Ava's Story)

Seattle Soulmates

Her List (Amalia and Axel Williamson)

McKinley's Obsession Duet

Josh and Emily's Story

Ruining Her

Ruining Him

Sick Love Duet

Unhinged Desires (Dominic McKinley and Lucy Christianson)

Certifiable Attraction (Dominic McKinley and Lucy Christianson)

The Valentino Empire

Devilish King (Holly and Theo's story)

Unassuming Queen (Holly and Theo's story)

United Reign (Holly and Theo's story)

Brutal Princess (Neo and Angelica's Story)

Reclaiming Lola (Lola and Dr James)

Sons of Valentino Series

Relentless Devil (Theo & Maddie's story)

Merciless Devil (Matteo & Savannah's story)

Soulless Devil (Romeo & Livvy's Story)

Reckless Devil (Luca & Katerina's Story)

A Valentino Reunion (The entire Valentino Family)

The Tempter Series

Following His Rules (Xavier & Shardonnay)

Following His Orders (Nathan &Bentley)

Following His Commands (Alistar & Dani)

Legacy of Valentino

Remorseless Devilette (Izzy and Mikhail)

Vengeful Devilette (Izzy and Mikhail)

Vancouver Knights Series

Break Out (Liam and Aliyah)

Know The Score (Grayson and Kathryn)

Light It Up Red (Travis and Liliana Valentino)

Puck Blocked (Luke and Montana)

De Bellis Crime Family

A Sinner's Promise (Gio and Eloise)

A Sinner's Lies (Gabe & Daisy)

A Sinner's Virtue (Marcel & Zoe)

A Sinner's Saint (Vin & Cammi)

A Sinner's Truth (Santo & Aria)

Club Omerta

Are you a part of the Club?

Don't want to wait for the next book to be released to the public?
Come and Club Omerta for an all access pass!

This includes:
• daily chapter reveals,
• first to see - everything, covers, teasers, blurbs
• Advanced reader copies of every book
• Bonus scenes from the characters you love!
• Video chats with me (Kylie Kent)
• and so much more

Click the link to be inducted to the club!!!

CLUB OMERTA

About the Author

About Kylie Kent

Kylie made the leap from kindergarten teacher to romance author, living out her dream to deliver sexy, always and forever romances. She loves a happily ever after story with tons of built-in steam.

She currently resides in Sydney, Australia and when she is not dreaming up the latest romance, she can be found spending time with her three children and her husband of twenty years, her very own real life instant-love.

Kylie loves to hear from her readers; you can reach her at: author.kylie.kent@gmail.com

Let's stay in touch, come and hang out in my readers group on Facebook, and follow me on instagram.